WISHES

P9-CBU-033

WISHES

WAKEFIELD PRESS
CAMBRIDGE, MASSACHUSETTS

GEORGES PEREC

TRANSLATED BY
MARA COLOGNE WYTHE-HALL

GEORGES PEREC

TRANSMOGRIFIED BY
MARA COLOGNE WYTHE-HALL

WISHES

WAKEFIELD PRESS
CAMBRIDGE, MASSACHUSETTS

This translation © 2018 Wakefield Press

Wakefield Press, P.O. Box 425645,
Cambridge, MA 02142

Originally published as *Vœux* © Editions du Seuil, 1989
Collection *La Librairie du XXIe siècle*, sous la direction de
Maurice Olender.

All rights reserved. No part of this book may be reproduced
in any form by any electronic or mechanical means (including
photocopying, recording, or information storage and retrieval)
without permission in writing from the publisher.

This book was set in Garamond Premier Pro
and Helvetica Neue LT Pro by Wakefield Press.
Printed and bound by McNaughton & Gunn, Inc.,
in the United States of America.

ISBN: 978-1-939663-33-7
Available through D.A.P./Distributed Art Publishers
75 Broad Street, Suite 630
New York, New York 10004
Tel: (212) 627-1999
Fax: (212) 627-9484

10 9 8 7 6 5 4 3 2 1

CONTENTS

Foreword by Maurice Olender   vii

Translator's Introduction   ix

WISHES • *Translation*

A LITTLE ILLUSTRATED ALPHABET PRIMER   1

WORKED-OVER COMMONPLACES   11

TRANSLATIONS FROM LATIN   21

THE ADVENTURES OF DIXION HARRY   31

FOOTNOTES TO MUSIC HISTORY   41

ANTHUMOUS WORKS   53

PLAYING ON THE BLUES: BRIEF ANTHOLOGY OF AMERICAN JAZZ   61

ROM POL   77

DICTIONARY OF FILMMAKERS   89

QUENEAU COCKTAIL   103

WISHES • *Transmogrification*

A LITTLE ILLUSTRATED ALPHABET PRIMER   127

WORKED-OVER COMMONPLACES   135

TRANSLATIONS FROM LATIN   139

THE ADVENTURES OF DIXION HARRY   147

FOOTNOTES TO MUSIC HISTORY   157

ANTHUMOUS WORKS   167

PLAYING ON THE BLUES: BRIEF ANTHOLOGY OF AMERICAN JAZZ   175

ROM POL   187

DICTIONARY OF FILMMAKERS   197

QUENEAU COCKTAIL   211

Between 1970 and 1982, the year of his vanishing, Georges Perec sent, almost every winter, his best *Wishes* to his friends for the New Year. These little albums are collected here in the order they were written.

In his "Approximate Bibliography (Accompanied by Some Comments by the Author)," published in facsimile in the *Cahiers Georges Perec* 1 by POL in 1985, Perec describes these compositions:

> *Wishes* (these are short texts, generally based on homophonic variations, printed in editions of about one hundred copies and sent to my friends on the occasion of the new year).

At the origin of each of these *Wishes* is a homogeneous set of utterances which Georges Perec borrows from the most familiar elements of culture: proverbs or clichés, names of filmmakers or famous musicians, titles of books or well-known films. From these he builds a dialogue, scene, or story. As with a pun, the similarity of the voicing opens the door to the unexpected. Placing himself among the descendents of Roussel, Queneau, and Leiris, Georges Perec "raises the pun to the level of punishment."[1]

These *Wishes*, which combine the spirit of play with the rigor of language, can now be discovered, one by one, as they were intended for their readers.

The publication of this volume was arranged by Éric Beaumatin and Marcel Bénabou, whom I warmly thank.

Maurice Olender

1. "Éleve le calembour à la hauteur d'un supplice": a "texticle" from the pen of Raymond Queneau's pseudonymous Sally Mara in her collection of "Foutaises."

TRANSLATOR'S INTRODUCTION

In the beginning was the pun.
—Samuel Beckett, *Murphy*

Meticulously silly, Georges Perec's *Wishes* demonstrates language's fundamental urge to never get to the point: the meaning of words has been subordinated to their sound, allowing these sounds in turn to generate new, often nonsensical, meanings. These overdetermined non sequiturs make an interesting contrast to the automatic writing of the Surrealists (the counterpoint to Perec and the Oulipo): whereas the unfettered imagination of automatism too often resulted in more a Surrealist style than an exploration (a style, moreover, that never quite escaped the iron grip of Lautréamont), Perec and his Oulipian colleagues sought ways to escape this snare through the use of structure and constraint.[1] They have on several occasions referred to themselves as defiantly "anti-chance." If a failure of automatic writing lies in the fact that the unconscious is ultimately more controlled than the Surrealists had hoped and conceived, the Oulipo avoid this problem by grounding their constraints in the arbitrary: their constraints are rigorous literary machines into which one can feed anything.

In the present volume, Perec fed the relatively simple mechanism of the pun with a series of lists. Placing himself in the tradition of literary listmakers (among whom he counted Rabelais, Jules Verne, and Michel Butor), Perec also managed to insert himself, as well as fellow Oulipian Raymond Queneau, into the very lists themselves (see "Wishes" 6 and 10). *Wishes* resembles his other works in its hints at self-inscription, and there are numerous details for obsessive readers of Perec to trace through to his other books.

Of what interest, though, are these texts to the "common" reader? This is a question that often arises with any employment of that lowest of humors, the pun. Even when spoken of in admiration, puns maintain this undignified status: "Punning . . . may be the lowest, but at all events is the most harmless, kind of wit," Coleridge once claimed, "because it never excites envy."[2] But this low form of culture, of obvious appeal to Perec, (who drew much from the base matter of everyday life),[3] has also been heralded by the likes of Georg Lichtenberg: "where the common people like puns and make them, the nation is on a high level of culture."[4]

But even these defenses don't always serve Perec's *Wishes* well. Jonathan Swift, in his "Modest Defence of Punning," launched his defense with an attempted distinction between "good" and "bad" puns. Such a distinction, though, has little to ground itself: the practice in itself is what is often deemed to be good or bad. If a distinction *is* to be made, it should perhaps be the one Walter Redfern has loosely made between "pointed" and "pointless" puns. A pointed pun, in which words are made to work overtime, creates something of a closed circuit: it is self-referential and complete. For Perec, however, homophony serves to generate narrative, not restrict it. Which is to say that words here are not just making love, they are procreating.

This brings the reader to one of the central questions that has divided Oulipians: once text has been generated, should it stand on its own, or should its generative methods be revealed? That is, should the value of Perec's *La Disparition* lie in the fact that it was written without the letter "E," or solely in the quality of its narrative? Although some of Perec's colleagues, such as Raymond Queneau and Harry Mathews, were either opposed to or simply uninterested in revealing the bones beneath their textual flesh, Perec was always ambivalent on the issue, and his ambivalence is evident in this volume. The "Commonplaces" ("Wish" 2) takes a stand by withholding its table from the reader, but it proved to be an anomaly in the series. The "Translations from Latin" of the following year half-expose their play in the pretransformed table at their end, but after that, Perec chose to expose his wordplay in all its glory.

In one of his later, collaborative projects, *Ellis Island*,[5] Perec related an account of a multilingual pun: an elderly Russian Jew, having just arrived at Ellis Island, is advised to choose an Americanized name to offer the immigration officers for their records. But when finally asked for his name, the Jew, having forgotten his previously chosen "Rockefeller," can only utter "schon vergessen [I've already forgotten]." His subsequent moniker: John Ferguson.

Generations of names, of words, the generation of language and the search of offspring for their linguistic roots . . . all a roundabout analogy for why a text might not always be interested in standing on its own; but also a reminder that even at their least serious, Perec's various works, major and minor, present a very disparate but quite unified whole.

●

I have made two translations of each pamphlet, the first one literal (which I've labeled as a "translation"), the second more of an adaptation working from the generative lists Perec used (which I've chosen to call, by way of distinction, a "transmogrification"). As Redfern claims in his book on puns, "the punster simultaneously begs for a pat on the back and dreads a punch on the nose":[6] I saw no reason to deny the reader either pleasure. Given the linguistic feats of Perec's other translators (obvious examples being Gilbert Adair and Ian Monk's respective lipogrammic renditions of *A Void* and *The Exeter Text*), I felt that rendering Perec without constraint would be shirking the ludic work at hand. Unfortunately, to present direct homophonic renditions of Perec's tables into English along with their semantic meaning is simply impossible. With the transmogrifications, I have instead replicated Perec's process and provided English equivalents of the homophonic tables (with the exception of the "Commonplaces," which provides no table). These equivalents were then used to generate the English texts; it is these that make up the second half of this book. The first half, then, provides the more literal translation of Perec's texts, with the English in brackets when wordplay demanded the impossible. The transmogrifications that make up the second half can be regarded as a "formal" translation: a translation that renders the play (rather than meaning) of Perec's text into English.[7]

It might be noticed that these formal English adaptations have almost tripled Perec's scatological forays (not to mention doubled his sexual allusions). While the translator is willing to stand accused of what Redfern calls "fart for fart's sake," it would be appropriate to misquote him in my defense: "There is an indissoluble link, if I may speak with a po-face, between punning and the number two."[8] Why do puns lend themselves so easily to such humor? Perhaps it would be best to end with Samuel Beckett, who spoke of his writing in terms that could also apply to *Wishes*: "My work is a matter of fundamental sounds (no pun intended)."[9]

●

I would like to thank Kevin Costa for his assistance on the Latin, Chris Eyer and Anthony Zannino for their contributions of two very pointed puns, Suzanne Gauch and Eugenio Rasio for their input on an earlier version of this translation, David Bellos and Charles Bernstein for their initial encouragement and support of this project, and Harry Mathews for his helpful reading of the first half of this manuscript. For this revised version, I would like to warmly thank Judy Feldmann for all her input and patience.

NOTES

1. The Oulipo, or the Ouvroir de Littérature Potentielle: a group of writers and mathematicians founded by Raymond Queneau and François Le Lionnais in 1960. Their work (and play) consists of the theory and practice of constraint as a means to literary production and inspiration.
2. Coleridge, *Seven Lectures on Shakespeare and Milton* (London: Chapman and Hall, 1856), 66.

3. Perec's own term for this stratum of lived experience was the "infra-ordinary."

4. Both Coleridge and Lichtenberg are quoted by Walter Redfern in *Puns* (Oxford: Blackwell, 1984), a work that has influenced this preface.

5. Translated by Harry Mathews and Jessica Blatt (New York: The New Press, 1995).

6. Redfern, *Puns*, 29.

7. I have adhered to Perec's game rules in both versions—as well as to their occasional suspensions. For the Oulipo, a true homophonic translation repeats no words from the initial transformation of the source text (that is, the text should not repeat any corresponding words from the table from which they are derived). For the most part, Perec seems to have exempted proper names from this rule, as many are repeated from table to text; he did not, however, limit his exceptions to them. Discounting the second and third booklets (whose tables do not allow for such an enumeration), Perec repeated a total of 141 words from table to text throughout these French texts; 69 of them are proper names. In my "formal" translations (the second half of this book), I repeat a total of 101 words, 29 of them proper names. Subtracting proper names from the totals of exceptions, we are left with a sum total of 72 instances of word repetition throughout either set of translations. I only mention this in case any excessive finickiness should take on the appearance of laziness.

8. Redfern, *Puns*, 22.

9. "No pun intended" is the punster's classic ad lib, which provides two things: a back door (should anyone catch the pun), as well as a pointer (should anyone happen to miss it). This brings us to a second dichotomy of the pun: the intended pun and the unintended. Continuing from Redfern's dichotomy, then, we have four distinctions of the pun (a "punnett square," if you will):

a. Intended Pointed	b. Unintended Pointed
d. Intended Pointless	c. Unintended Pointless

Thus we have (a) the intended and pointed pun: the low humor of common wit (for example, "A boiled egg every morning is hard to beat"); (b) the unintended and pointed pun: the Freudian pun, or "slip" ("A Freudian slip is when you say one thing and mean your mother" being a category *a* pun describing category *b*); and, for literary purposes, the more fruitful variations of the pointless pun: (c) the unintended and pointless pun of the Surrealists (who were better known for the visual pun, as in the paintings of Salvador Dalí and René Magritte, but in language was exemplified by someone like Robert Desnos: "En nattant les cheveux du silence / six lance / percent mes pensées en attendant [While braiding the hair of silence / six spears / meanwhile pierce my thoughts]"; and (d) the intended and pointless pun of Perec and the Oulipo.

WISHES

TRANSLATION

●

1970

A LITTLE ILLUSTRATED ALPHABET PRIMER

At the Moulin d'Andé

MCMLXIX

1

Before the Christmas window display of a large shop, a small child is expressing his skepticism or dislike for the majority of its toys, and points to the one he would like to receive: a magnificent bicycle whose shape curiously evokes the first vehicles of this sort.

2

In a living room, some wives chatter about adultery.

3

A young child, raised by an English family, notices, somewhat mischievously, that his father is often described as "podgy."

4

A young fife player of the Navy Service Corps Band has deserted and taken refuge at the home of a friend wine grower. But the police arrive. The wine grower quickly orders the deserter to toss his fife and identity papers into one of the casks in his cellar.

5

One day, while playing with his friends, Guy had to run with the utmost urgency to the john. It became a joke with his gang to remind him of this incident.

6

Though overwhelmed by his lot, this man does not allow himself to get demoralized; he has already collapsed, he explains, so he's reached the limit.

7

After many years of journeying, we finally sighted it, the little isle whose bookish descriptions we knew so well.

A French musician from the end of the nineteenth century is reading, with a slight anachronism, one of Thomas Mann's last novels.

8

One of the heirs to the Maison Mame, the great Catholic library at Tours, became the student of Marcel Marceau: this metamorphosis might surprise some people.

I have a kind of kneading trough at home that moves about when I talk in a hushed voice.

9

Young Antoinette, fondly nicknamed Nanne, greatly admires the sestina, and more particularly the general theory—or N-ina—of these types of poems.[1]

10

While traveling to Cremona, the supreme Pontiff anxiously scans the malodorous river.

The Russian priest gives his son something to drink, but the boy isn't thirsty; he wants to play horsey on his father's shoulders.

11

A passerby remarks how exceptional it is to hear people laugh in the street.

12

A bashful mason hides in order to bring his plaster buckets up to his companion who, exasperated, orders him to stop fussing about.

A linguist wonders, laughing, if Saussure's theories form a valid sieve.

13

Though discreetly questioned by the US Ambassador, the head of the Yugoslavian State did not wish to reveal his intentions.

14

Go on! Be headstrong! Shout your fits of enthusiasm to the world!

15

Although a former polytechnician, this government official bitterly reflects that he has achieved nothing but a modest post in the Department of Labor on Avenue de Saxe, and tells himself that, if he had to do it over again, he would choose another path.

16

Although she has not quite yet learned how to speak, Helen Keller would like to ask for something from her servant Zacherie, familiarly called Za. But finding it too difficult, she gives up, exasperated.

TABLE

1.   **BAH! BEH! BI BEAU: BUT**
       [Bah! Beh! Beautiful Bi: objective]
2.   **CAQUET: QUI COCU?**
       [Gossip: who's a cuckold?]
3.   **DAD EST DIT DODU**
       [Dad is called chubby]
4.   **FAF' ET FIFRE AU FÛT!**
       [ID papers and fife on tap!]
5.   **GAG: EH, GUY, GOGUES HUE!**
       [Gag: Hey, Guy, toilet ho!]
6.   **JA J'AI GÎT, JAUGE EU**
       [In sooth I laid, gauge was]
7.   **LÀ L'EST, L'ÎLOT LU**
       [There it is, the read-of islet]
     LALO LIT L'ÉLU
       [Lalo reads *The Holy Sinner*]
8.   **MAME ET MIME, OH MUE!**
       [Mame and mime, oh transformation!]
     MA MAIE, MI-MOT, MUE
       [My dough trough, hushed, moults]
9.   **NANNE: N-INE AUX NUES**
       [Nanne: N-ina praised to the skies]
10. **PAPE ÉPIE, PÔ PUE**
       [Pope keeps a lookout, Po stinks]
     PAS PÉPIE, POPE, HUE
       [Not parched, priest, gee up!]
11. **RARE EST RIRE AUX RUES**
       [Rare is laughter in the streets]

12. **ÇA CESSE, HISSE AU SU!**
    [That's gotta stop, heave ho openly!]
    SAS EST-CE, HI, SAUSSURE?
    [Is it a sieve, hee, Saussure?]
13. **TÂTÉ, TITO TUT**
    [Tested, Tito silent]
14. **VA! VEUX! VIVE AU VU!**
    [Go! Desire! Live in view!]
15. **QU'SAXE, EX-X! OH QUE SU . . .!**
    [Only Saxe, ex-student of the École Polytechnique! Oh, to have known . . .!]
16. **ZA, Z'ÉZIZ . . . AU ZUT!**
    [Za, I'se zee . . . oh drat!]

100 copies of this
"Little Illustrated Alphabet Primer"
were stenciled for my friends
on the occasion of the new year

with my best wishes
for nineteen hundred and seventy

1972

WORKED-OVER COMMONPLACES

1

When still a child and playing the English horn, Taine was one day fascinated by the view of a cluster of islands in the distance that seemed to be approaching him like ships driven by a slow anger.

This vision engrossed him to such an extent that he was taken off guard by a barrel, which hurtled down on him and swallowed him up.

2

Once upon a time there was a plump paver's beetle.

In reality, it was a fairy, at least at its birth.

And thanks to it, leprosy ceased to hold sway for a while.

3

A ski merchant had two sons. The younger was sensible and looked after the shop, but the elder was often subject to violent fits of insanity in the course of which he would demolish everything.

One day the merchant had to leave on a journey and advised his younger son to keep him informed on the course of business.

No sooner had he left than the elder son burst into the shop, obviously victim to one of his dreadful attacks. Fearing for the stock, the younger son tried to throw his brother out, but the elder possessed colossal strength and the shop was soon strewn with bits and pieces of skis.

His heart heavy, the younger son found himself obliged to telegraph his father that all the skis were broken and that the older brother was still there!

4

I've had it!
Every day I have to flatter more and more slavishly!
I make hems and prepare the poultry!

But in the meantime, nothing shall be denied my nieces' violinists!

5

A very curious thing happened to the people of Évreux:
One morning, they woke up with their bodies completely coated in a substance that came from either a neighboring lake or from the Pole.
After investigation, it appeared that those responsible had to be sought in the United States, and more precisely, at Yale.

6

Advice for a young stag:
The stag party was cleansed of anything that might have been impure.
If you want to grow wings, provoke the contact of the years.

7

I didn't understand this custom that consists of fastening horsehair to the bottom ends of shrouds.
I asked the leading seaman, a good fellow of Auvergne origin, for an explanation.
He replied in his flavorsome accent:

"That, you big ninny, is so that, after the sea spray has lashed at them all night and the icy wind of the dawn has made them hard as rock, one can know what side the wind's coming from!"

8

It is known that Holland's fortune rests on two basic institutions: Herring Fishing and the Drainage of the Lowlands (constantly menaced by the Waters).

A shrewd mountebank had the ingenious idea to extol both at the same time.

He managed to tame a herring by feeding it exclusively on rapeseed.

Thereafter, as soon as it sees some rapeseed, the herring rushes over and snaps it up. Then, to show its gratitude, it leaps out of the water and breaks through a paper drum as a banderole unfurls from its tail, praising the construction of dikes.

9

For its heroic conduct on the battlefield, the whole battalion was blessed by the chaplain, and this blessing earned it its nickname.

One of this battalion's survivors, Yves, became a traveling perfume merchant. He goes from village to village in a peculiar automobile, the back of which he has specially adjusted in order to lay out his stock of perfumery.

He occasionally works with a colleague, but this time, he came on his own.

10

I once wanted to take a job as a woodcutter in Scotland.

"What will my wages be?" I asked.

"Your only salary," I was told, "will be to go 'HUH' before cutting down your tree."

"Fuck that!" I replied (rather crudely, I admit). "I at least want a pleated skirt and a blanket in the style of your country!"

11

Everyone knows that the famous blue jeans retailer, Levi, made his fortune by flooding the supermarkets of the Paris region with his product.

This led to an unfortunate experience for a young girl of Beauvais named Yvette. For as becoming as blue jeans may be, they don't protect very well against the cold and the rain, and young Yvette today suffers from a chronic catarrh and coughs incessantly.

One day she caught sight of the aforementioned Levi inaugurating one of his most up-to-date sales outlets, and she could not refrain from hurling abuse at him.

The affair made some noise. The papers spoke of it. It is comforting to note that the region sided entirely with Yvette.

12

This man is most certainly ill. He has vomited everywhere. I bring his attention to the fact that people are walking through his vomit.

This seems to disconcert him at first. Then, all of a sudden and for no apparent reason, he is astonished by those masses of light hairnets worn by the young dancers of the Opéra.

13

A famous soccer champion can be recognized in this photo.

On the station platform, he is meeting, deeply moved and happy, a compatriot whom he has not seen in years.

One may notice a curious detail: although, given his weak chest, this soccer player never travels without an enormous scarf, he has, on this occasion, left it at home.

14

IF, WHEN THE DAY DRAWS TO A CLOSE,
SOME GRAVE ATTACK OCCURS,

IS IT AN ABSOLUTE SCANDAL,
OR IS IT THE DAY THAT IS CROOKED?

15

I wrote to the one I love:

Move your antique bicycles,
And point out the way North to the one who asks,
And do like Hans and decorate the pigs' hairs!

And may all that be the sign of the love you bear for me!

16

Letter to several stupid individuals:

You pack of idiots!

You got it all wrong! That Grecian bowl was used exclusively for the ball game the Athenians loved to play.

The two teams got in a circle and began to play. When the game grew particularly fierce, a supporter of one of the sides would always be found in the audience who would then manage to offer the aforementioned bowl, obviously filled with cheap wine, to one of the opponents. Which of course influenced the outcome of the game!

That's what that bowl was used for, you ignoramuses!

I was told:

"Give up this deplorable habit you've picked up of belching!"

I replied:

"Do you mean to say that the Great Pan is responsible for this inextricable miscellany that my texts have become?

TABLE

THIS TIME, THERE IS NO TABLE.

ONE MUST START ACCEPTING
THAT A TEXT CAN STAND
ON ITS OWN.

these "Worked-over Commonplaces"
were devised
and realized at the end of the year
nineteen hundred and seventy-one
for the new year

accept them with my best wishes

1973

TRANSLATIONS FROM LATIN

Regarding the curtain calls that virtuosos regularly get from concertgoers, it should be noted that it is less the artist's haste that prompts them than the way he wears tails and the expression on his face.

Buddy, your chick ain't nothing but a shapeless blob. But buddy, when you take her from behind, your family jewels sure give her one hell of a steamy session.

Léa, she wanted t'chat. I told her:
    "Léa, if you want to chat, come find me at the Estonian villa!"

To whom can we attribute this painting depicting a nun whom, in the ancestral dwelling of the Pitts, a young sailor is in the midst of robbing?

The one on whom we wanted to take revenge had fled to Bray. We went in pursuit, but a tire burst. We had to put the car on a jack, undo the wheel, and change it.
    "Hurry up, boys," our chief told us, "we're on his heels!" And as I hadn't yet screwed the nuts and bolts back on, he ordered me to do so.

Fantômas laughs at Juve: "That takes the cake," he says to him, "you're sent to Dacia, but the Dacians must have given you a scare—you don't exactly seem in a hurry to get there!"

Lacking all hope for love, a man came to ask me for some help.
  I say to him:
  "Bring this gold up from the cellar to the attic."
  He asks me:
  "Does that really answer to the bitterness I feel toward women?"

OPEN LETTER TO THE EX-SECRETARY-GENERAL OF THE UNITED NATIONS:

You're skinny: you've been reduced to cooking sixteen of your blazons to accompany your rice! You laugh, but you ain't decent!

What's the matter with this little fellow? Does he think a trident reserved for adults is made of gold?

May it be understood by all, for I ordain and decree it so, that in elevated residences, the unity of work raises the unit of electrical resistance!

One day, a novice cook wanted to impress his master: he set about preparing a piece of butchery by blending a stream of violently beaten vinegar into it.
  But the master cook was not impressed: "My dear friend," he says to him, "your vinegar's no good; by precipitating it thus, you only turn it into mold. Use this cut of meat to prepare some brawn or some bottom round instead."

One day, an explorer was giving a lecture on his expedition to King Solomon's mines.

"...it was only on the following day," he was recounting before his mesmerized audience, "that we reached the mines..."

Upon uttering these last two words, he sensed he was going to catch fleas.

Curie is stupid and fatigued, and the pile driver under which he is standing is agitated by abrupt movements similar to hiccups. Even so, this man has had an erection since daybreak.

I had demonstrated the need for the metro. The decision was up to Vinci, a fierce partisan for the bus. I went to see him. I thought I could convince him, but his haughty reception left me distraught and he stubbornly clung to his opinion.

When the artist has decided to take things to their limit, to risk his all, his art can resemble that of the cowboy who tries to remain as long as possible astride a wild bull.

GOSH DARN IT! THE PRODUCTS WEREN'T BLENDED: MY SOUFFLÉ ISN'T RISING!!!

"You seem depressed, why don't you go see a Japanese play? I'm sure it would do you good."

I went.

"So?"

"Of course, the function of great Japanese theater is to bring people together and unite..."

"Didn't I tell you so?"

"But I was so beside myself..."

The daughter of Marshal Douglas Haig is named Odette and she has some disgusting habits: when she wants to get spruced up, she asks her two friends—one named Hérode and the other Hussein—to cover her with rotten eggs! They're right in the middle of doing so: I'd hold your breath if I were you!

I have an etching at home: on the left, a woman disguised as the young count de La Fère is dismissing the accusation made against her; on the right, a seated silhouette—in which one recognizes the writer Eugène Sue, a half-human gray mass that could evoke an ass walking along the banks of the Rhine—asks a man a question that he, although a champion, cannot answer.

IS IT ONLY ON CORPSES THAT ONE CAN SEE A SMALL AUREOLE APPEAR NEAR THE TEMPLES?

"Ah! You know that Aimé finally landed a job?"
   "No kidding! An interesting one?"
   "You must be joking! A job as a flunkey: he spends his time making clodhoppers!"

HE'S HOPELESS IN MATHEMATICS BECAUSE HE'S BEEN CORRUPTED BY THE WINE OF ASTI!

Odette is convinced that the people in the neighborhood assemble in militias; she has even counted six of them. But, I explained to her, the situation is worse than that: these militias are only the pretext for the formation of veritable leagues, each of which could group together two militias.

A pervert asked me if he could be cured of his perversions.

   I told this man:

   "Discover love, become a priest, and bugger off!"

O county town of the Maritime Alps, what are you but a useless source of trivial words?

You discovered an utterly original type of poem: an ode made of a succession of witticisms; but you're doing nothing with this discovery. Devote yourself to it more thoroughly! Give it all the fame it deserves and ask one of your students to write his thesis on the subject!

What a stroke of luck: Yves just asked me to fasten a paver's beetle with a screw!

We were sauntering about in Nantes. At a certain moment, we let loose some resounding farts.

   One of us was assailed by remorse. He recalls this episode in his dreams and wakes up shrieking.

His scream haunts him. Suffering and fatigue have dried up his speech.

By threatening this man with a blackjack, the circus manager forces him to change into a dwarf as small as Tom Thumb. You should see the haste with which he climbs up the little pole!

TABLE

ABYSSUS ABYSSUM INVOCAT *ad augusta per angusta* ALEA JACTA EST aquila non capit muscas ARS LONGA VITA BREVIS *audaces fortuna juvat* AURI SACRA FAMES ave Caesar morituri te salutant CASTIGAT RIDENDO MORES *cogito ergo sum* FLUCTUAT NEC MERGITUR homo homini lupus IBANT OBSCURI SOLA SUB NOCTE *labor omnia vincit improbus* LARVATUS PRODEO mens sana in corpore sano NOLI ME TANGERE *numero Deus impare gaudet* O FORTUNATOS NIMIUM SUA SI BONA NORINT AGRICOLAS o tempora o mores PANEM ET CIRCENSES *qui bene amat bene castigat* SIMILIS SIMILI GAUDET si vis pacem para bellum SUPER FLUMINA BABYLONIS *timeo Danaos et dona ferentes* VENI VIDI VICI verba volant scripta manent VULNERANT OMNES ULTIMA NECAT

these "Translations from Latin"
were devised and realized
at the end of the year
nineteen hundred and seventy-two

one hundred copies were printed

with my best wishes
for nineteen hundred and seventy-three

1975

THE ADVENTURES
OF
DIXION HARRY²

ALL'S WELL THAT ENDS WELL

In homage to Lewis Carroll, I named my cow Alice. She drops her calf as the devil, completely intoxicated, calls out to her.

A STITCH IN TIME SAVES NINE

A few of us jumped the wall of the boarding school we were attending for our primary studies. We strolled over to the flea market when we caught sight of one of our teachers in the crowd looking for secondhand goods. We were about to skedaddle when one of us noticed that, luckily, it was the only one of our teachers who wasn't a brute, a young German romanticist whom we had nicknamed Heine.

A THING OF BEAUTY IS A JOY FOR EVER

and may my paraph have the shape of an egg: sphere that shall be my implement!

is that the source of my knowledge?

may our Picardy "yes" be vigorous and forever young!

TO BE OR NOT TO BE

I like you very much, Renaud, but really, you have no memory, you really have no memory.

ALL ROADS LEAD TO ROME

We know Sertorius' arrogant assertion:

> *Rome is no longer Rome,*
> *It is everywhere I am!*

What is less known is that Sertorius, prefiguring the anaerobic Incroyables, wrote his name this way in Greek:

$$\Sigma\varepsilon\tau o\iota\upsilon\varsigma$$

DON'T COUNT THE CHICKEN BEFORE THEY ARE HATCHED

You were so humiliated that you no longer dare use the calculator. Don't worry about it: calculate by instinct. Your aversion will wear off; don't just demand support—get it.

IF AT FIRST YOU DON'T SUCCEED, TRY, TRY AGAIN

To Rodrigue:

What's this! What am I hearing? This man wants to plunge you into a bath of internal secretions to turn you into a Redskin! Laugh at yourself! Laugh at yourself and cover him!

DON'T PUT YOUR EGGS ALL IN ONE BASKET

You are so ashamed that you feel minuscule next to these bedded down-and-outs who push you away. But don't go begging for despicable gibes!

TOO MANY COOKS SPOIL THE BROTH

The tailor exaggerates. That takes the cake. I dust everywhere, but he only looks after the clothes of this guy named Paul.

EVERY DOG HAS HIS DAY

Degas liked his model Eve very much; but she was usually sullen and complained at the drop of a hat. She especially hated the sun. That explains this photograph in which one sees her laughing her head off while the painter raises a piece of light material over her head, which four slender poles are going to hold up.

DON'T CROSS YOUR BRIDGES BEFORE YOU'VE COME TO THEM

Distended by these turpitudes from which fetters reemerge, I cross out, but Pierre Jean Jouve erases everything, down to the slightest meaningful element.

LESS HASTE MORE SPEED

You love gold.
    You think gold is tasteful.
    It's your main topic of conversation.

But I think it's horrible.

PEOPLE IN GLASS HOUSES SHOULD NOT THROW STONES

Letter to Pauline:

You're telling me how worried you are over the cottage you visited. But it's much worse than you think. All the mirrors there are covered and the cabbages from the vegetable garden prove that they're breeding bad horses. You are absolutely right to grumble!

MANY HANDS MAKE LIGHT WORK

Submitting to his wife's desires, this man rubbed his entire body with garlic. This demonstrated an ignorance of this plant's virulence that, contrary to what he was looking for, completely gnawed away his genitals!

MAKE HAY WHILE SUN SHINES

There is absolutely no reason that some fellow and a churchy old man should do each other in . . .

EVERY CLOUD HAS A SILVER LINING

I have two Scandinavian friends, both very superstitious: Eve and Inge. On a statue of one of their most ancient divinities, they found a nail that they hung on a thread. Inge asks me why Eve is so delighted. I tell her that nothing gives Eve greater pleasure than to see the nail swing on the end of its thread, especially when it points to the clove of garlic that, for fear of vampires, they hung over their bed.

HE LAUGHS LAST LAUGHS LONGER

On this island, emaciated and exhausted by fighting, it is difficult to stay clean. Wash up, but you have to take things as they come!

IT NEVER RAINS BUT IT POURS

This ruthless bandit operates in the forest of Painpont, not far from Rennes. But the day on which I came to see him, he had only come upon one traveler and his loot was just one meager purse.

A BIRD IN THE HAND IS WORTH TWO IN THE BUSH

My ship is blocking the harbor. The port is at my mercy. To be on the safe side, I decide to dine on board. But Han d'Islande is letting me know he's attacking and that he's going to get through even so. And what's more, he's succeeding!

OPEN THE DOOR AND SEE ALL THE PEOPLE

O, Paule, such is my distress: my sleep is a succession of sharp and deep points and there is no crueler game.

NEVER GIVE A SUCKER AN EVEN CHANCE

Around 21:00, I decided to leave. I went like a soul in pain through the covered markets of the Medina when—O joy—Anne came to join me.

TABLE

ALICE VÊLE; SATAN, SOÛL, HÈLE
> [Alice calves: Satan, drunk, hails]

INSTIT' CHINE: TAILLE. MAIS C'EST—VEINE—HEINE
> [Teach' hunting for antiques: split. But it's—luck—Heine]

ET SIGNE OVE, BILLE-OUTIL. Y SAIS-JE? OÏL FORT ET VERT
> [And egg-shaped mark, ball-tool. I know from it? Strong and spry *Oïl*]

T'OUBLIES, Ô, RENAUD, T'OUBLIES
> [You forget, O Renaud, you forget]

OÙ LES «RHO» S'ÉLIDENT: TOUT ROME
> [Where the "rho" elide: all Rome]

D'HONTE, COMPTE DE CHIC; HAINE SE BIFFE: FORCE ET ARRACHE AIDE
> [From shame, count from memory; hatred crosses itself out: force and grab aid]

I' VA T'FAIRE SIOUX DANS DU SUC, CID! TE RAILLE, TE RAILLE ET GAINE!
> ['E's gonna make you Sioux in some juices, Cid! Jeer at yourself, jeer at yourself and sheath!]

D'HONTE PETIT, OÙ RAYENT GUEUX AU LIT. NE VANNES BASSES QUÊTE
> [From shame little one, where beggars lash out in bed. Don't seek low jibes]

TOUT D'MÊME, I COUD QUE CE PAUL! JE BROSSE!
> [Even so 'e only sews this Paul! I brush!]

ÈVE RIT: DEGAS HISSE DAIS
> [Eve laughs: Degas hauls up canopy]

D'HONTE GROSSIE OÙ REBRIDENT. JE BIFFE OR JOUVE GOMME TOUT SÈME
> [Fattened by shame that restricts. I cross out whereas Jouve erases every last character]

LAID C'EST CE THÈME: OR SAPIDE

[Wretched is this theme: sapid gold]

PIS, PAULINE: GLACES À HOUSSES, CHOUX DÉNOTENT ROSSES. TONNE!

[Worse, Pauline: mirrors with covers, cabbages indicate nags. Inveigh!]

MAIS NIANT DE CE MEC, L'AIL DÉVORE QUEUE

[But denying this guy, the garlic devours prick]

MEC ET OUAILLE SE N'ÉCHINENT

[Guy and one of the flock don't wear each other out]

ÈVE RIT: CLOU D'ASE OSCILLE VERS L'AIL, INGE

[Eve laughs: nail of Ase swings toward the garlic, Inge]

ILE HÂVE, LASSE: TE LAVE SELON GUERRE

[Gaunt isle, weary: wash yourself accordingly]

I' T'NAIT VERS RENNES PETITE BOURSE

['E had near Rennes little purse]

A BORD DÎNÉ-JE. HAN DIT «JE FORCE TOUT»: I' M'DÉBOUCHE!

[Aboard dined I. Han says "I'm taking it all by force": 'e's unblocking me!]

Ô PEINE, JE DORS DENTS DE SCIE. Ô LE JEU PIS, PAULE

[O sorrow, I sleep jagged. O the worst game, Paule]

NEUF HEURS! J'Y VAIS; SOUK ERRE. ANNE Y VINT, D'CHANCE!

[Nine o'clock! I went; souk wanders. Anne came, luckily!]

these twenty-one homophonic
paraphrases were devised
and realized in the first
days of December 1974
at
Griffydam (Leicestershire)

one hundred guppies
were printed

receive them
with my best wishes for
nineteen hundred and seventy-five

1977

FOOTNOTES TO MUSIC HISTORY

1

"I'm telling you, you'll never manage to reinforce this confusion of laths with scraps of bone!"

"And how should I have known that?"

"You could have read it in *Madame Bovary*, straight from the mouth of Monsieur Homais."

2

I've been studying long enough.

I've had it!

I'm gonna get my bac!

3

As I was leaving, I heard one of my pals say: "'e may be taking off, but 'is gas sure ain't!"

4

I have an original recipe for making beautiful candles: I take some barley, I fry it, and I mix it with rice.

5

I've long wanted to give my girlfriend a coarse-grained silk fabric. But I haven't had the courage.

Today, I'm finally determined to do it.

6

A dissident disciple of Oldenburg and Christo, Mose worked for a long time on a piece that he called *The Clan of the Wolves*, which evoked the terrible Chicago gangland killings of the Prohibition.

This masterpiece's final form was a gigantic heap of corpses wrapped up in what morgue workers call "meat sacks."

7

It is often asked why Indians shut themselves up in their tents, crowding in a circle around their fires.

That comes from their superstitious fear of a carnivore who would leap without fail like a vampire onto their carotids to suck out all their blood!

8

One night, I wanted to enter the home of a certain lady who occupies my thoughts, named Bérénice, known more familiarly as Ber.

She was afflicted with a very jealous husband who frequently suffered from an excessive and chronic loss of voice.

I was in the place, and the lady was leaving the conjugal bedroom, when the affair came to a sudden end—for the spouse, waking up with a start, inquired in an inaudible voice after the absence of his wife!

9

Another anecdote concerning this charming Bérénice: her husband always wants to make her eat cabbage!

10

That gives her gas!
of course, says the husband,
with all those cabbages!

11

WHEN A WORK
IS WEALTHY
IT'S OFTEN BECAUSE
ITS ENERGY IS WOOLLY

12

Where can I lie down to die?

Observe the color of your farts: when you see one turn green, lie down and die, for you've found your place.

13

When people of the East see urbanites brag on the snow-covered pistes, they always kindly advise them to act like the center of attention *after* they've taken off their skis.

14

"I want to eat Jacques," a cannibal tells me.
     "Do you at least have a barrel?"
     "You betcha."
     "A big barrel?"
     "Bigger than a cask."
     "OK, then."

15

So then make
          a poem
on what gave a stronger
          taste
to the bosoms
          of these singers

16

If you see a corpse lifting a root vegetable, don't hesitate to call for help.

17

"Do it by hand!" That's easy for you to say: you know perfectly well that putting the machine on MANUAL always makes for botched jobs!

18

I called the boss. I told him that the delivery had been made; I added that the traffic was making for more and more darned problems. At that moment, the call was cut off . . .

19

How lovely she is when she puts that big barrette on her little hat!

20

Am I this professional's only servant when he is on his estate??

21

Really, when you were a wrestler in Italy, it made you laugh?

22

goodness!!
what's with me??
I'm lemon-colored!!

23

Stir your stumps! Put away the merchandise Eugene sent us!

24

Bah!
     I'm never going back to Lipp's!
     The reception there is icy, you leave refrigerated!

Bah!
     Reading doesn't get you anywhere!
     Stop reading so much!
     Get stoned instead—go on, don't be afraid!

TABLE

1. **D'HOMAIS, NIE QU'OS CARRENT LATTIS**
   [From Homais, deny that bone squares lathing]

2. **J'EN SAIS BASTE! J'TIENS BAC!**
   [Never mind I know it! I'm gonna have the bac!]

3. **GEORGE FILE: I PÈTE ET L'ÉMANE**
   [George is dashing off: 'e farts and emanates it]

4. **J'AI ORGE FRIT DE RIZ: CHANDELLE**
   [I have barley fried with rice: candle]

5. **J'OSE ET FAILLE DONNE**
   [I dare and give faille]

6. **WOLF GANG: AMAS DES HOUSSES: MOSE'S ART!**
   [Wolf Gang: pile of stretch covers: Mose's art!]

7. **LOUP DE WIGWAM: BÊTE AUX VEINES**
   [Wigwam wolf: beast at veins]

8. **CAR LE MARI APHONE: «OÙ EST BER?»**
   [Because the aphonic husband: "Where is Ber?"]

9. **PRENDS CE CHOU, BER!**
   [Take this cabbage, Ber!]

10. **ROTS, BER? CHOU-MANNE!**
    [Belches, Ber? Cabbage-manna!]

11. **RICHE ART, VAGUE NERF**
    [Rich art, vague nerve]

12. **GIS OÙ CE PET VERDIT**
    [Lie where that fart turns green]

13. **MOT D'EST: MOUSSE HORS SKI**
    [Word of the East: Puff up outside ski]

14. **EN TONNE, DÉVORE JACQUES**
    [In tun, devour Jacques]

15. **RIME CE QUI CORSA COFFRES**
    [Write verse on what spiced up chests]

16. **MORT HISSE RAVE? HÈLE!**
    [Dead man hoists root vegetable? Hail!]

17. **«MANUEL» DES FAILLES A**
    ["Manuel" flaws has]

18. **HÉ QUE TORTS VILLE. . . ALLO, BOSS?**
    [Well faults city . . . Hello, Boss?]

19. **BELLE À BARRE TOQUE**
    [Beautiful with bar hat]

20. **SERS-JE PRO QU'AU FIEF?**
    [I serve pro only at fief?]

21. **À ROME, CATCHAS-TU RIANT?**
    [At Rome, you wrestled laughing?]

22. **JAUNE QU'AI-JE?**
    [Yellow what's with me?]

23. **GARE LE STOCK À EUGÈNE!**
    [Store Eugene's stock!]

24. **FI! LIPP GLACE!**
    [Pooh! Lipp chills!]

25. **FI! LIS PEU, DROGUE OSE!**
    [Pooh! Read little, drug dare!]

these "Footnotes to Music History"
were realized at the end of the year
nineteen hundred and seventy-six

100 copies were printed
numbered from
197700 to 197799

1978

ANTHUMOUS WORKS

1

What should one say to a girl intimidated by fellatio?

2

Because Queen Westfarthing was farting all the time, King Westfarthing had no court. Three courtiers, exasperated by the situation, decided to carry on regardless. It matters little if the queen farts, they said, so long as the court exists. The first of these courtiers was named Yves, the second Éloa, the third, Guy, who later on provided the inspiration for Shakespeare's character, Romeo. Thus the chronicler was able to write:

3

Attila had a warrior named Kyd, who had the tiresome habit of entering his leader's tent at any given moment, forcing the latter to shout each time:

4

An Englishwoman and a Frenchman one day made a double wager: the stakes for the first one being 10,000 pounds sterling, that of the second, a simple meal at Taillevent's. Yet it was stipulated that the two wagers were intertwined: one could not win one without winning the other. And when the Frenchman learned that he had won the first bet and lost the second, he cried out grievously:

5

When an American cop has reached the summit of his career, he has nothing more to do but look after himself:

6

In times past, dreams obsessed their dreamers. But since then, they have been thoroughly examined by psychoanalysis, and one can now say that henceforth, never again:

7

To welcome Sadate and Begin, Carter had a canopy set up at Camp David, and gave the same key to the two heads of state that allowed them access to any room. The columnists naturally wondered about the significance of these two gestures:

8

Who still recalls the prophecy of this preacher of Hull (England), who promised his flock that their city shall experience a biblical fate?

9

The European tour of the great Canadian polo team, the "Sovereigns" of the Mounties, gave rise to numerous scandals. The "Sovs," as the press and the general public call them, owed their victory to a particular stratagem:

every time they came to the opposing goal, they made their horses whinny in such a way that the goalkeeper, terrorized, completely cracked up. The behavior was soon judged to be irregular and the "Sovs" and their horses were imprisoned. Fearing a spectacular escape, the head warden even had additional bolts installed. In vain, for, using their famous technique, the "Sovs" had no difficulty in smashing through the doors of their cells:

10

It is known that to compile their guidebook, Gault and Millau proceeded in this manner: Gault went from restaurant to restaurant and telegraphed his meals to Millau who, staying in Paris, would write up the corresponding notes. It is in this way that Gault, after having eaten some monkfish and young wild boar's head at the hôtel du Lac at Issoudun, sent off the telegram:

11

You want to know something? Al Capone was a complete imbecile, not to mention conceited as hell:

12

In his inaugural lecture at the Collège de France, the critic X brilliantly brought the fundamental break of today's novel to light: on the one hand, the legacy of Henry James, and on the other, that of Boris Vian, a profound alternative, which he summed up in a formula that remains famous:

13

At the dental school library, the shelves bear printed notices specifying the nature of the books classed upon them. The shelves on which the works treating dental pains are located are obviously overloaded and dangerously sagging:

TABLE

1. **LÈCHE, OSE**
   [Lick, dare]
   Les Choses

2. **QU'ELLE PÈTE! YVES, ÉLOA, GUY (DONC ROMÉO) FONDENT LA COUR!**
   [Can she fart! Yves, Éloa, Guy (thus Romeo) found the court!]
   Quel petit vélo à guidon chromé au fond de la cour?

3. **HUN NOMMÉ KYD, HORS!**
   [Hun named Kyd, out!]
   Un Homme qui dort

4. **LADY, CE PARI SCIONS!**
   [Lady, let's saw this wager!]
   La Disparition

5. **L'ABOUTI COP SE CURE**
   [The accomplished cop scrapes himself clean]
   La Boutique obscure

6. **LES RÊVES N'HANTENT**
   [Dreams don't haunt]
   Les Revenentes

7. **EST-CE PAIX, CE DAIS, CE PASSE?**
   [Is it peace, this canopy, this master key?]
   Espèces d'espaces

8. **HULL SERA SION**
   [Hull shall be Zion]
   Ulcérations

9. **DOUBLÉS VERROUS, LES «SOUV» HENNIRENT ET ENFONCENT**
   [Double bolted, the "Sovs" whinny and smash through]
   W ou le souvenir d'enfance

10. **LAC: LOTTE, HURE**
   [Lac: Monkfish, boar head]
   La Clôture

11. **AL, FAT BÊTE**
   [Al, smug fool]
   Alphabets

12. **JAMES OU VIAN**
   [James or Vian]
   Je me souviens

13. **L'AVIS «MAUX DE DENTS» PLOIE**
   [The notice "Teeth pains" bends]
   La Vie mode d'emploi

"Although not published in the form of wishes, there is an obvious parallel between 'Anthumous Works'—which was partially published in *Magazine littéraire* in October 1978—and those texts" (Georges Perec, in *L'Arc*, n. 76, 1979, 94).

1979

PLAYING ON THE BLUES

Brief Anthology
of
American Jazz

JULIEN "CANNONBALL" ADDERLY

A musician was asked where he had learned to play.

"In the virgin forest," he said, "thanks to a magic liana that would stammer out songs and broadcast radio programs!"

LOUIS ARMSTRONG

My ear can be dangerous: once it goes into action, it's all I need to completely nibble you up!

COUNT BASIE

May the prince reigning at Tunis cut the roots of this humiliating dishonor!

SIDNEY BECHET

One day an avant-garde director put on a *Cid* in which he made Rodrigue a sort of Godot. But the critics, of course, didn't like it.

BIX BEIDERBECKE

A titled businessman was famed for diversifying his products: ballpoint pens, cigarette lighters, disposable razors, as well as for sponsoring daring navigators; these days he takes an interest in antique musical instruments, minstrel violins in particular.

BARNEY BIGARD

The Prime Minister is certainly a hard man, but you can't compare him to a paratroop colonel!

CLIFFORD BROWN

It has long been asked what the significance was of these intaglio strokes that seem to spring up from the arm of such-and-such figure on some of the Parthenon's frescos. An archaeologist has proposed a rather attractive explanation: these figures would be the builders and the engraved lines would symbolize their *ell*, that basic measurement on which all ancient architecture is founded.

DAVE BRUBECK

"I hate my son's wife! In the first place, she's frightfully skinny!"
    "If it's of any consolation, tell yourself that she's what makes you eat . . ."

KENNY CLARKE

On the day after her trial, Cauchon paid a visit to Joan in her cell.
    "It's not you at whom I'm enraged," he told her. "My hatred is not directed at Joan, but at the Arc that you've dared raise against us!"

JOHN COLTRANE

I know a man who roams relentlessly, roams without respite. He is always dressed in an old frock coat and wears what was once a white detachable collar, now yellowed by the years.

MILES DAVIS

What difference is there between AMORA mustard and MAILLE mustard?

None whatsoever, save that you pull the lid off of one, whereas the other one unscrews.

DUKE ELLINGTON

A party renegade tries to persuade one of his cellmates:

"Don't believe what your leaders tell you! Get angry! Ask them just what the Party stands for!"

ELLA FITZGERALD

A woman is complaining in a maternity ward. She wanted a son, but the woman next to her is the one who had one, whereas she gave birth to a daughter.

ERROL GARNER

Seek Adventure! But seek it where even the Visionary dare not go!

STAN GETZ

Menaced by the terrible flies of sleeping sickness, a donkey escaped them through a clever stratagem: he started turning somersaults, which entertained the flies to such an extent that they stopped thinking of biting him.

DIZZY GILLESPIE

"How can I discreetly let this man know we had the same analyst?"
   "Did your analyst have any distinguishing marks?"
   "Not as far as I know. Ah, yes! He was very proud of his cardigans."
   "There you are, then! You have a simple password."

BENNY GOODMAN

Is there anything better in the world than the miraculous food sent to the Hebrews in the Desert?

COLEMAN HAWKINS

Workshop 15 is a sad affair. Because glue is manufactured there and it gives off toxic smells.

WOODY HERMAN

Those Hebrews weren't the only ones who were saved by Manna. Others knew a miracle of the same sort: they crossed an arid desert on which nothing sprouted except for clumps of holly. But on the following day, the holly turned into bread!

JAY JAY JOHNSON

One day, an extraordinary bird showed up in the countryside. Although it resembled a jay, it was yellow, completely yellow. For weeks, our hounds chased this golden bird. And when I managed to catch it, I said to the bugler accompanying me:

"You can sound the horn, I've finally caught it!"

PHILLY JO JONES

A dishonest fabric dealer was using doctored ells. But he was terribly afraid of the Inspector who would sometimes come to check whether or not the ells were complying with regulations: consequently, he had an accomplice who warned him in advance and allowed him to take off!

ROLAND KIRK

For the opening of his cafe, an owner offered everyone there a *blanc-cassis*.

The following day, the entire city was stinking of it and there was another mob at the café door.

LEE KONITZ

Did Taoism make its way into the Russian church? No: a recently discovered painting on wood clearly shows that the Rites of the Orient had rejected the word of Lao-Tzu.

GENE KRUPA

They wanted me to believe in the Existence of God. But it was useless.

THELONIOUS MONK

The story of William Tell is actually very different from what legend relates. In fact, William Tell missed the apple and killed his son.

Scorned by all and chased out of every town, William Tell wanted to redeem himself at all costs. One day, some villagers, mocking him but also feeling some pity, set down an old cover on a post and challenged him to hit it. William aimed, shot, but, unlucky indeed, missed this target, as large as it was.

GERRY MULLIGAN

"I just wrote a poem, but I'm looking for a rhyme for the word 'Tzigane.'"

"Have you thought of Polish hoodlums?"

"Hell's bells! You're right!"

CHARLIE PARKER

I once attended a reading by René Char. At first, I thought he was reading, but I soon realized that his eyes weren't even looking at the lines of the book set on the table, and that he definitely knew his poems.

OSCAR PETTIFORD

"Did you see that bus!"

"It was really tiny!"

"I wonder what make it is?"

"Look, it's a Ford!"

BUD POWELL

A biologist has just pulled off a remarkably successful experiment: a birth *in vitro*, carried out, not on an intact animal, but on a little piece of dermis!

SONNY ROLLINS

It's not always pleasant to agree to act in an overly trendy play. But even so, you'd have to be an unrefined imbecile to refuse!

CURLEY RUSSELL

A man who wanted to become a bibliophile asked me for some advice.

"Try," I told him, "by hook or by crook, to procure first editions of Raymond Roussel."

HORACE SILVER

If you leave, if you go seeking Adventure, go to the spirits of the air!

ZUTTY SINGLETON

A musician came to jam in a nightclub. The others got ready to accompany him, but they soon stopped, disappointed and a bit scandalized. For the musician knew nothing about jazz; he wasn't playing in tune—he was only trying to make it seem like he was!

WILLIE SMITH "THE LION"

One of my friends, a specialist in myths and popular traditions, had to give a lecture.

"I just finished a work," he told me, "on the Seine's tributaries. Did you know that the riverside residents of the Yonne offer their river an unparalleled allegiance? I would like to read to the audience the pages that I'm devoting to this curious myth. What do you think?"

"That's a very good idea," I replied.

CECIL TAYLOR

The abbé Faria gave not only the secret of Monte Cristo to Edmond Dantès, but that of four other islands also overflowing with treasures. And he asked him to keep these secrets under his hat.

LENNIE TRISTANO

What is sadder than a nest fallen from a tree: this wreath of twigs in which no birdie shall ever again dwell?

FATS WALLER

The fashion designer Jacques Fath was known for never being on time for social gatherings; but one evening he couldn't have been more punctual: one should add, though, that on that day, he was dead drunk!

COOTIE WILLIAMS

A worker priest made this declaration to me:
"I wasn't assembling the congregation about my Faith in my cassock. But my dungarees sure unite them!"

LESTER YOUNG

One day, Freud made a completely Freudian slip. He was having a discussion with Jung and Ferenczi: Ferenczi was doing all of the talking, and Freud wanted to ask him to let the other speak a little. But he did exactly the opposite!

KEITH JARRETT

Huh? What's going on? I screwed up the alphabetical order! It's really time for me to quit!

TABLE

J'EUS LIANA QU'ÂNONNE BALLADES ET RELAIE
  [I had liana that recites ballads in a fumbling manner and relays]

L'OUÏE S'ARME ET JE TE RONGE!
  [The hearing arms itself and I gnaw away at you!]

QU'HONTE BEY SCIE!
  [May shame Bey saw off!]

CID N'EST BECKETT
  [Cid isn't Beckett]

BIC SE BAILLE DES REBECS
  [Bic gives way to rebecs]

BARRE N'EST BIGEARD
  [Barre isn't Bigeard]

GLYPHES HORS DES BRAS: AUNES
  [Glyphs out of arms: ells]

D'HÂVE BRU, BECTE!
  [From gaunt daughter-in-law, nosh!]

QU'HAINE NE NIE QUE L'ARC!
  [May hatred only repudiate the Arc!]

JAUNE COL TRAÎNE
  [Yellow collar roams]

MAILLE SE DÉVISSE
  [Maille unscrews]

DIS: OÙ QU'EST LIGNE? TONNE!
  [Say: Wherever is line? Inveigh!]

ELLE A FILS, JE RÂLE
  [She has son, I groan]

ERRE OÙ L'HAGARD N'ERRE
  [Wander where the wild-eyed one doesn't wander]

GEORGES PEREC

CET ÂNE ÉGAIE TSÉ-TSÉ

[This ass amuses tze-tze]

DIS-Y: GILET «PSY»

[Say this: cardigan "shrink"]

BÉNI GOÛT DE MANNE

[Blessed taste of manna]

COLLE ÉMANE AU QUINZE

[Glue emanates from Fifteen]

HOUX D'HIER: MANNE

[Holly of yesterday: manna]

J'AI GEAI JAUNE: SONNE!

[I have yellow jay: sound!]

FILE, Y JAUGE AUNES!

[Take off, sizing up ells!]

RELENT DE KIR: QUEUE

[Stench of Kir: line]

L'ICÔNE NIE TSEU

[The icon denies Tzu]

JE NE CRUS PAS

[I didn't believe]

TELL HONNI HOUSSE MANQUE

[Despised Tell misses cover]

J'AI RIME: HOOLIGAN!

[I have rhyme: Hooligan!]

CHAR LIT PAR CŒUR

[Char reads by heart]

OH, CE CAR PETIT? FORD!

[Oh, this little car? Ford!]

BOUT DE PEAU VÊLE

[Scrap of skin calves]

SOT NIE RÔLE «IN»

[Idiot denies "in" role]

COURS LES ROUSSEL

[Seek out Roussels]

HORS, À CES SYLPHES ERRE

[Out, to those sylphs roam]

ZUT, Y SINGE LE TON!

    [Shoot, he's aping the tone!]

OUI, LIS CE MYTHE: ZÈLE À YONNE!

    [Yes, read this myth: zeal for Yonne!]

CES ÎLES, TAIS L'OR

    [These isles, hush up the gold]

LE NID, TRISTE ANNEAU

    [The nest, sad ring]

FATH, SOÛL, À L'HEURE

    [Fath, drunk, on time]

COUTIL, OUI, LIE ÂMES

    [Dwill, yes, unites souls]

LAISSE TAIRE JUNG!

    [Let Jung shut up!]

QU'EST-CE? J'ARRÊTE!

    [What the—? I'm stopping!]

these forty homophonic variations
were composed
at Fief Naton
on 1 January 1979

100 copies were printed

with my best wishes
for nineteen hundred and seventy-nine

1980

ROM
POL³

CARTER BROWN JOHN DICKSON CARR RAYMOND
CHANDLER LESLIE CHARTERIS JAMES HADLEY CHASE
PETER CHEYNEY AGATHA CHRISTIE ARTHUR CONAN
DOYLE IAN FLEMING ERLE STANLEY GARDNER WILLIAM
GOODIS DASHIELL HAMMETT PATRICIA HIGHSMITH
CHESTER HIMES WILLIAM IRISH MAURICE LEBLANC
GASTON LEROUX HORACE MAC COY ELLERY QUEEN
DOROTHY SAYERS MICKEY SPILLANE STANISLAS ANDRE
STEEMAN REX STOUT JIM THOMPSON SS VAN DINE

1

A very small young man was apprenticed to a fabric dealer. When he saw him, the latter couldn't help smiling.

"At any rate," he told him, "you won't need a ruler to measure the rolls: with your arms spread, you make exactly one ell!"

2

"What are you muttering about now?"

"I'm not talking to you, I'm talking to my clock."

"To your clock! Why's that?"

"Because I can't wait for the quarter hour to ring!"

3

In the first version of his *Requiem*, Arconati had intended the finale to be performed by the four soloists. But when the soprano read the score, she was so furious that she insisted the composer cross out her entire part!

4

Stop reading detective novels all the time! Discover René Char! Don't get discouraged!

5

Don't talk to me of Knoll, Thonet, or Charles Eames. When I'm sitting down, what I prefer are really ghastly seats!

6

Give off wind,
Push the wagonettes
to the depth of the mine
and come into the world!

7

With the aid of his plane, the Muslim leader of the Ismailian sect of India and Pakistan leveled the little pedestal on which he wanted to set his golf ball, and which, given his wealth, is cut from a diamond.

8

Toward the end of the twelfth century, a wealthy resident of Toulouse sent his nephew to study in Picardy. Don't bother coming back (he told him) if you don't know how to at least speak the awful dialect they use around there!

9

It is well known that all the emperors of the Ming dynasty were exceptionally corpulent. But the biggest of them all was Hi.

10

You don't have to stay unfailingly at your post like the guardsmen. If you want to leave the stand, do so, and set off for adventure!

11

How right you are, my dear Édouard, says the director of the Paris Opera to Lalo, to seek your inspiration in this legendary city of Brittany that was suddenly swallowed up!

12

They were so fed up with shepherd's pie that as soon as they saw that they were going to be served one, they took off!

13

A young postal worker, dedicated to sorting, wanted to know when he had to break off work. He was told:

"As long as it's just letters arriving, you should of course sort them, but as soon as you start seeing cloves of garlic appearing in the mail, then you should stop!"

14

Invited to a costume ball at the home of the author of *Drames de Paris*, Théophile Gautier and Carlotta Grisi dress up, he as Argus, and she as the nymph Io.

"Now don't forget," repeated Gautier to his companion, "as soon as you walk in, you moo!"

15

You're probably right to want to bump into your wealthiest friends.

16

When Othello made his triumphant return to Venice, the Doge granted him the only privilege no other foreigner had ever been able to obtain: that of replacing the black flag, which signified a state of emergency, with the immaculate banner of Victory atop the great flagpole of San Marco.

17

When you prepare a butter- and flour-based sauce and it doesn't take on an attractive appearance, one thing you can try is to thin it down with water, the way a plasterer would.

18

When questioned as to which races she preferred, Madame Bovary always said that she only had esteem for those who—in France—were North of the Loire.

19

My girlfriend is passionately interested in Georges Bernanos's novel, *Monsieur Ouine.*

She no doubt reads many other books, but she never rereads any but that one.

20

Evoke past times!
Recall the gold and silk
Of which those former days
Were woven!

21

An overly greedy donkey one day approached a big lump of bread and swallowed it down, paying no heed to the crust. His punishment for this infamy has yet to end.

22

This burro is much too overworked to serve you as a beast of burden: settle for making it carry the souls of your ancestors!

23

You're not allowed to consider the balls you sent outside the boundaries of the court as wins. You have to cross them out from your score.

24

Perched on the shoulder of a horn player, a mulish macaw was endeavoring to imitate the human voice. And when it succeeded in doing so, it asked him to celebrate its achievement by blowing into his instrument.

25

At a garden party, wonderful victuals had been arranged in those flat-bottomed baskets called winnowing baskets; and I urged a timid friend to go serve himself.

1. ÉCARTE LES BRAS: AUNE
    [Spread your arms: ell]
2. JE NE DIS QUE: SONNE, QUART!
    [I'm only saying: ring, quarter hour!]
3. RAYE MON CHANT DE L'AIR!
    [Score out my aria song!]
4. LAISSE, LIS CHAR, T'HÉRISSE!
    [Drop it, read Char, get your back up!]
5. J'AIME ÇA, DE LAIDES CHAISES
    [I like them, ugly chairs]
6. PÈTE, HERSCHE, ET NAIS!
    [Fart, haul coal, and be born!]
7. AGA TAQUE RICHE TEE
    [Aga plane rich tee]
8. AU RETOUR, CONNAIS LANGUE D'OÏL
    [Coming back, know northern French]
9. HI, ENFLÉ MING
    [Hi, swollen Ming]
10. ERRE, LAISSE STAND, LES GARDES N'ERRENT
    [Roam, leave stand, the guards don't roam]
11. OUI, LIE ÂME AU GOUT D'YS
    [Yes, unite soul to the liking for Ys]
12. D'HACHIS ELLES LES METTENT
    [From mince they take off]
13. PAS TRI SI AIL S'IMMISCE
    [No sorting if garlic interferes]

14. **CHEZ CE TERRAIL: MEUH!**
    [At this Terrail's: Moo!]

15. **OUI, LIE AMIS RICHES**
    [Yes, bind rich friends]

16. **MAURE, HISSE LE BLANC**
    [Moor, raise the white]

17. **GÂCHE TON LAID ROUX**
    [Temper your ugly roux]

18. **AUX RACES, EMMA QU'OÏL**
    [As to races, Emma only Oïl]

19. **ELLE RELIT QU'OUINE**
    [She only rereads *Ouine*]

20. **D'OR, Ô TISSER HIER!**
    [Of gold, O weave yesterday!]

21. **MIE QU'EXPIE L'ÂNE**
    [Soft part of bread for which the ass atones]

22. **CET ÂNE, I S'LASSE, EN DRESSE TES MÂNES**
    [This ass, it's tired, train it for your manes]

23. **RAYE CE QUE T'AS «OUT»**
    [Score out what you have "out"]

24. **J'IMITE HOMME, SONNE!**
    [I mimic man, sound!]

25. **ESSAIE CE VAN, DÎNE!**
    [Try this winnowing basket, dine!]

these twenty-five homophonic variations
were realized at the end of the year
nineteen hundred and seventy-nine

150 copies were printed

with my best wishes
for nineteen hundred and eighty

1981

DICTIONARY
OF
FILMMAKERS

ALEXANDRE NEWSKY
[Alexander Nevsky]

AMARCORD

L'AVVENTURA

LA CAPTIVE AUX YEUX CLAIRS
[The Big Sky]

CELUI PAR QUI LE SCANDALE ARRIVE
[Home From the Hill]

CET OBSCUR OBJET DU DÉSIR
[That Obscure Object of Desire]

LE CIEL EST À VOUS
[The Woman Who Dared]

CITIZEN KANE

LA COMTESSE AUX PIEDS NUS
[The Barefoot Comtessa]

LES DEMOISELLES DE ROCHEFORT
[The Young Girls of Rochefort]

LE DERNIER TANGO À PARIS
[Last Tango in Paris]

DOCTOR JERRY AND MISTER LOVE
[The Nutty Professor]

DOUX OISEAU DE JEUNESSE
[Sweet Bird of Youth]

HIROSHIMA MON AMOUR

IRÈNE ET SA FOLIE

LES JEUX DE LA COMTESSE DOLINGEN DE GRATZ
[The Games of Countess Dolingen]

JOHNNY GUITAR

THE MAN WHO SHOT LIBERTY VALANCE

LES MARIÉS DE L'AN II
[The Married Couple of the Year Two]

LE MÉCANO DE LA GENERAL
[The General]

LE MIRAGE DE LA VIE
[Imitation of Life]

NORTH BY NORTHWEST

LA NUIT TOUS LES CHATS SONT GRIS
[At Night All Cats Are Crazy]

OBJECTIVE, BURMA!

RENCONTRES DU TROISIÈME TYPE
[Close Encounters of the Third Kind]

SINGIN' IN THE RAIN

LA SIRÈNE DU MISSISSIPI
[Mississippi Mermaid]

SI VERSAILLES M'ÉTAIT CONTÉ
[Royal Affairs in Versailles]

TEMPÊTE À WASHINGTON
[Advise & Consent]

LE TESTAMENT DU DOCTEUR CORDELIER
[The Doctor's Horrible Experiment]

LE TRÉSOR DE LA SIERRA MADRE
[The Treasure of the Sierra Madre]

TROIS HEURES DIX POUR YUMA
[3:10 to Yuma]

MICHELANGELO ANTONIONI

The four Sundays preceding Christmas shall be murderous.

BERNARDO BERTOLUCCI

After lunching at Lipp's, Gault and Millau squabble over the check. Millau finally proposes a wager:

"Let's go look downstairs; if that silly dodo Hallier is there, I'm paying; if not, you are."

"Okey doke," said Gault.

So they go down and, of course, Hallier is there.

CATHERINE BINET

As he was getting ready to sign an edict, Henry IV noticed that his quill was splotching. He was brought another, which he tried out on a blank piece of vellum by quickly writing the words "Year of Grace" twice over. Kept by a secretary with foresight, this vellum became an extremely rare autograph.

Having learned that it was for sale, I offered its owner a manuscript of the troubadour Eudes d'Angerville as a first installment. We came to an agreement and settled upon a rendezvous. But as I went there, I wondered if I had indeed brought the aforementioned MS with me.

RICHARD BROOKS

When he was little, Rudolf Hess said that he had a zoo. In actual fact, he only looked after a dozen geese.

LUIS BUÑUEL

Louis-Philippe received as a present from the dey of Algiers three black oxen that he considered to be too skinny, and which he sent to graze at La Bourboule. Various calamities immediately swept down upon the kingdom of France.

The astrologer Christomontanus was consulted, and he ordered the king to immediately stop this fattening that was contrary to ritual.

DELMER DAVES

"The central voice of the French Communist Party is rubbish," said Irina.
    "Rotten!" added Natasha.
    "Putrid," went Masha, going one better.

JACQUES DEMY

Who do I see in the distance, coming to meet me? My friends Denis, Maurice, and Jean-Paul. I call out to them in a loud voice, but emotion is distorting my face!

STANLEY DONEN

Having written a threatening letter to Victoria, the anarchist Guy asked his leader how he should close it.

"Just put your first name," the latter replied, "and add: he who brings bad luck to monarchs!"

SERGEI EISENSTEIN

There is nothing finer in the world, says certain Chinese recipe, than this river fish related to the perch, when one prepares it with birds' nests.

FEDERICO FELLINI

When Chilperic, king of the Lombards, died, his four sons divided up his property: Gondebaud took the goats, Théodéric the sacred vessels, and Béowulf the women; as for Mark, he put himself at the head of the horde and set off to pillage Noricum and Rhaetia.

JOHN FORD

At the *Foire du trône*, Big Bertha challenges the gawking onlookers to bind her, hand and foot, as swiftly as her partner, Hans. No one manages to do so, save for a few Tziganes not in the competition who do as well as he.

JEAN GRÉMILLON

You've spent your life studying the history of the New Haven University and that of the duke of Auerstaedt. It's time you moved on to something else!

SACHA GUITRY

"You want some coffee?"
    "Of course I want some coffee."
    "Here's your coffee!"
    "Hey! You're burning me! You nuts or what?!?"

HOWARD HAWKS

An old cowboy is educating a greenhorn:

"When a storm is about to break, follow the young calves; they always go where the sky is cloudless."

ALFRED HITCHCOCK

This contract is rotten! Not only should you not respect it, you should even contest it!

JOHN HUSTON

For the final battle scenes in *Star Wars*, George Lucas wanted electronic crossbows. Several special-effects experts proposed somewhat sophisticated lasers. But only one was clever enough to get his to function.

BUSTER KEATON

To say that Mr. Kane is uncomfortable is an understatement, Orson Welles explains to his producers; he's much more than uncomfortable: he's actually dying.

JERRY LEWIS

At the age of six, Henri Poincaré astounded his teachers by maintaining that, to calculate the volume of an ovoid, it is sufficient to set down as a principle that it is equal to the volume of a hemisphere.

JOSEPH MANKIEWICZ

Everyone knows the very charming Princess Hopi. What is less known is that she has a distant cousin who bears the same name as her, but she only has the rank of countess and always goes for a stroll in her birthday suit.

VINCENTE MINNELLI

You want to know what to do if the Indians attack?
Close the doors, decorate the wine bottles, and go to the riverbank to declaim poems!

OTTO PREMINGER

An inventor perfected a bovine washing machine. It's a sort of tub that starts working as soon as you slip a token into the appropriate slot.

BERNARD QUEYSANNE

At the end of her life, Sappho marries a king. But rather than take charge of the kingdom's affairs, she devotes herself to reading.

JEAN-PAUL RAPPENEAU

While visiting the little town of Eu, in Normandy, Madame Bovary made fun of its inhabitants, whose slowness is proverbial.

NICHOLAS RAY

How does one recognize a nonstriker? He leaves the factory much later than the others.

JEAN RENOIR

So she could illegally embark on a Turkish liner, a woman gave her suitor the responsibility of binding hand and foot the guard who was keeping a watch on the quay. But he proved to be incapable of doing so.

ALAIN RESNAIS

Mona, you're no longer in the prime of youth, and a certain stage of your digestion gets you very angry!

DOUGLAS SIRK

As he was making a portrait of a prince of the Persian Gulf, a painter imagined a pneumatic device that, to give a tint to his drawing, could forcefully project a mixture of water and sepia.

STEVEN SPIELBERG

Before becoming a producer, Arthur Rank was a harness racer. But he didn't stay one for long. He took too much pleasure in getting tips, and his reputation was quickly tarnished on the racecourses.

FRANÇOIS TRUFFAUT

A young hippy who was getting married went to see her guru to learn how to play the reed pipe. She soon knew how to play the scale.

"How much do I owe you?" she asked.

"For *do*, *mi*, *fa*, and *sol*, that will be one hundred dollars each," said the guru.

"And for the other three notes?"

"They're my wedding present."

RAOUL WALSH

"What's this object?" I asked an American, pointing to a sort of plaque covered with livid grooves.

"It's my mother's—she's not very robust, but when she's drunk, she claws at it with all her might!"

ORSON WELLES

Don't think that Zen Buddhism is a school of kindness. On the contrary.

GÉRARD ZINGG

When the Russians took over Budapest, a group of conspirators circulated a message urging the Hungarians to drive them out: the signal for the rebellion would be some lengthy braying.

TABLE

L'AVENT TUERA
> [The Advent will kill]

L'EDERN Y ÉTANT, GAULT A PARI
> [Edern being there, Gault has wager]

L'AI-JE, EUDES, L'ACOMPTE À CES DEUX LIGNES «AN DE GRÂCE»?
> [Do I have it, Eudes, the down payment for those two lines "Year of Grace"?]

DOUZE OIES, ZOO DE JEUNE HESS
> [Twelve geese, young Hess's zoo]

STOPPE CURE AUX BŒUFS JAIS DU DEY, SIRE!
> [Halt course of treatment of jet oxen of the Dey, Sire!]

TROIS SŒURS DISENT: POURRIE HUMA!
> [Three sisters say: Rotten Huma!]

LAID D'EMOI, J'HÈLE DEUX ROCHE ET FAURE
> [Ugly from excitement, I hail two Roches and Faure]

SIGNE: GUY, GUIGNE DES REINES
> [Sign: Guy, rotten luck of the queens]

AH, LES SANDRES AUX NIDS, EXQUIS!
> [Ah, pike perches with nests, exquisite!]

A MARK: HORDE
> [To Mark: horde]

DES MANOUCHES OUT LIENT BERTHE ET VALENT HANS
> [Some gypsies bound Bertha and are worth Hans]

LAISSE YALE ET DAVOUT
> [Drop Yale and Davout]

SI, VERSE! AÏE! MAIS T'ES CON, TÉ!
> [Yes, pour! Ouch! But yer stupid, aintcha!]

LÀ QU'Y A P'TITS VEAUX, CIEUX CLAIRS
> [There, where there's lil' cows, clear skies]

GEORGES PEREC

N'HONORE CE BAIL, N'HONORE OU ESTE
[Don't honor this lease, don't honor or go to court]

LE TRAIT SORT DE LASER À MADRÉ
[The arrow leaves the crafty one's laser]

LE MEC KANE, AU-DELÀ DE LA GÊNE, EST RÂLE
[This guy Kane, beyond discomfort, is death rattle]

D'AUTOR, J'ÉRIGE EN DEMI-SPHÈRE L'OVE
[On my own, I establish in half-sphere the ovum]

LA COMTESSE HOPI EST NUE
[The countess Hopi is naked]

CÈLE HUIS, PARE KILS ET SCANDE À LA RIVE
[Conceal doors, bedeck cheap wine and chant at the bank]

TREMPETTE À VACHE: UN JETON
[Quick cow dip: a token]

IL RÈGNE ET SAPHO LIT
[He reigns and Sappho reads]

L'EMMA RIAIT DES LENTS D'EU
[Emma was laughing at the slow ones of Eu]

JAUNE, IL QUITTE TARD
[Scab, he leaves late]

L'ÉTAIT, CET AMANT DU DOCK TURC, HORS DE LIER
[He was, that Turkish dock lover, beyond binding]

IRE AU CHYME, AH, MONA MÛRE
[Ire at chyme, ah, Mona matures]

L'ÉMIR À JET DE LAVIS
[The emir through jet of wash-drawing]

RANK, HONTE DU TROT ASSIS, AIME «TIPS»
[Rank, shame of seated trotting, loves "tips"]

LA SI RÉ N'EST DÛ, MISSIS HIPPIE
[La si re isn't owed, Missus Hippy]

OBJET QUE CHÉTIVE, BUE, RAIE MÂ
[Object which puny, drunken, Ma scratches]

SI T'ES ZEN, QU'HAINE
[If you are Zen, only hatred]

L'ÂNE OUÏ, TU LES CHASSES, HONGRIE!
[The donkey heard, you drive them out, Hungary!]

these thirty-two homophonic variations
were worked out
in the first months of the year
nineteen hundred and eighty-one

some 200 copies were printed

receive them with my best
(if tardy) wishes
for the new year

1982

**QUENEAU
COCKTAIL**

At the OuLiPo
We prefer
The cocktails of Queneau[†]
To the quenelles of Cocteau

† A "Queneau cocktail" is a mixture of bitter San Pellegrino and Schwepps.

THIRTY-SEVEN TITLES

BÂTONS, CHIFFRES ET LETTRES

BATTRE LA CAMPAGNE

CENT MILLE MILLIARDS DE POÈMES

LE CHANT DU STYRÈNE

CHÊNE ET CHIEN

LE CHIEN À LA MANDOLINE

LE CHIENDENT

COURIR LES RUES

LES DERNIERS JOURS

LE DIMANCHE DE LA VIE

LES ENFANTS DU LIMON

EXERCICES DE STYLE

FENDRE LES FLOTS

LES FLEURS BLEUES

LES FONDEMENTS DE LA LITTÉRATURE D'APRÈS DAVID HILBERT

GUEULE DE PIERRE

LES IAUX[4]

L'INSTANT FATAL

LE JOURNAL INTIME DE SALLY MARA

LOIN DE RUEIL

MORALE ÉLÉMENTAIRE

ODILE

ON EST TOUJOURS TROP BON AVEC LES FEMMES

PETITE COSMOGONIE PORTATIVE

PIERROT MON AMI

POUR UN ART POÉTIQUE

LA RELATION X PREND Y POUR Z

SAINT GLINGLIN

SALLY PLUS INTIME

SI TU T'IMAGINES

SUR LES SUITES S-ADDITIVES

UN CONTE À VOTRE FAÇON

UNE HISTOIRE MODÈLE

UN RUDE HIVER

LE VOL D'ICARE

LE VOYAGE EN GRÈCE

ZAZIE DANS LE MÉTRO

GEORGES PEREC

1

A Champion Apprentice's Disappointment

The guy shows up in a sports club.

"What can you do?" asks the coach.

"I'm a judoka."

"Black belt?"

"Yup . . ."

"Sixth dan?"

"Oh, no no."

"Fifth dan?"

"Oh, not even."

"Then what?"

"Er . . . first dan."

The coach looks him up and down and shakes his head.

"First dan's not enough for my team."

2

On the Road

A miserable wretch is roaming along the road. Not only is he lacking in looks, but the disappointment that can be read upon his face makes him even uglier.

3

Explorers of the Lost Ziggurat

When Leonard Wooley arrived with his team at El-Muqayyar in 1922, he plunged with unconcealed enthusiasm into an excavation that the workers had just brought to light. He soon dragged himself out, though, bent in two by a piercing hernial pain, and asked before passing out:
"Have I finally found Abraham's homeland?"

4

This Man is Boring

Poison Ivy, *Dames Don't Care*, Caution and Callaghan, I find all of that rather flat, overrated, and frankly, a deadly bore!

5

First Reactions to Roosevelt

When, in 1933, the new president of the United States of America made public the measures he was introducing in the struggle against the crisis, the same cry, skeptical among Republicans, enthusiastic among Democrats, came from every breast.

6

Course in Elementary Geology

How is it that fossils of obviously aquatic livestock can be found upon a high mountain? Voltaire claimed they were the remains of the shells of the pilgrims going to Compostela. But his explanation only makes us smile today. The truth is that there once was a stream in the same spot that one day dried up, but whose bed, mixed and mashed up for thousands and thousands of years, ended up becoming a mountain.

7

Modest Proposal to the Minister for the Arts

To restore some sense of our most exalted national values to our youth, could we not, on certain occasions—14 July for example—equip the beautiful sculpted group known as *The Marseillaise* with a device so that stirring poetry would seem to emerge from the great open mouth of the winged and helmeted woman?

8

Pictorial Tastes of a Famous Model

When Mona Lisa was asked who her favorite painter was, she replied, to everyone's general amazement, that she put Della Francesca above anyone.

9

Eye for an Eye, Gadfly for a Gadfly

"What should I do?" Hera asked her older sister. "That dirty pig Zeus got some with one of my priestesses and to shield her from my righteous wrath, thought it good to transform her into a heifer. I demanded that she be given over to me and had her put under the guard of he who has so many eyes that he can never close all of them at once. But my vile spouse sent Hermes to knock him off. What can I do now? Change this little scumbag Hermes into a purse, or take it out on my husband?"

"Neither," replied Hestia the Impassive. "If you have to hurt someone, it should be the little cow who robbed you of your boyfriend's affection. Inflict her with a gadfly for all Eternity . . ."

10

The Twilight of the Gods

As they were administering him the Extreme Unction, the dying man sat up and, in a final burst of fanaticism, saluted his Führer.

11

The Extinction of Pauperism

In his attempt to put his social program into practice, Napoleon III sent for an economist and asked him how to do away with the poor.

The economist remained skeptical.

"A poor wretch will always be a poor wretch, unless, of course, one manages to cure him with a still."

12

Scandal at Saint-Germain-des-Prés

At the cafe Le Bonaparte, a customer is kicking up a fuss.

The manager is summoned.

"I am a passionate lover of yogurt," vociferated the fellow, "but what you've just served me is spoilt!"

"What? How's that!" exclaimed the manager, surprised. "But you can see for yourself the date written on the lid of the jar: this yogurt shows every indication that it's fresh!"

"That may be!" thundered the customer. "But I'm telling you, it's revolting and inedible!"

13

History of Antipsychiatry

In the beginning of the sixties, Laing and Cooper were discussing ideas that were to soon nourish the antipsychiatric movement.

"We must," Laing was saying, "denounce the idea of a single self."

"You're right, Ronald," replied Cooper, "you have to denounce this old concept of Unity!"

14

Education of a Wrestler

Al Fawbett, the famous wrestling champion whom his admirers nicknamed "The Fat" owing to his tremendous obesity, asks me to explain the difference between linen and nylon.

"Nylon has no elasticity, old boy, whereas linen is supple. That's their main difference!"

15

Morality and Cinema

When *Duck Soup* was released, puritanical societies wanted to have the film banned, claiming that it would corrupt the youth.

"But don't you understand," exclaimed a critic, "that if the Marx Brothers, and even more so the one among them who doesn't utter a word, start to become moralistic, they'll turn to shit!?"

16

A Tournament in Heaven

To relieve his tenants of their boredom, God arranges a go tournament in Heaven. Livy is in charge of forming one of the teams. One of his protégés, Cosimo de Medicis, proves to be a brilliant player and reaches the semifinals.

The game starts out fairly well for Cosimo. But Livy soon gets into a panic. His champion is apparently plunging into the trap set by his opponent and he hastily disposes several stones that seem intended to form an exit as hasty as it is inefficacious!

God (who sees all) reassures Livy:

"Calm down," he tells him. "Medicis knows very well that in go, there is no swift solution!"

17

Fain to Find a Fond Fan

A speleologist had descended to the depths of a cave, without any temporal indicator, and was wondering with some anxiety whether he would manage to hold out as long as Michel Siffre.

He obviously believed himself to be alone in the cave. But after a few hours or days, he encountered a being who, though not at all human, was no less likeable for all that and they immediately hit it off. And soon he asked his odd companion to aid him in shattering the record his predecessor had set.

18

How He Wrote Certain of His Books, 1

Raymond Roussel was asked why, in the capital of Ponukele, the week only has six days, from Tuesday to Sunday.

"There is probably no first day of the week in this country of Africa," he replied. "On the other hand, they're not lacking in the most famous of Guerlain's perfumes."

19

Torments of a Triumphant Collector

"What should I do to celebrate my acquisition of the last drawing that I had needed to complete my collection of the cartoonist Mittelberg's complete works?"

"Gordon's Dry is essential," I replied.

20

Curious Eating Habits of a Primate

Lily is a charming little female monkey whose progress in grammar has many a time astounded the most eminent psycholinguists. But she feeds herself exclusively on drawings executed with a mixture of water and sepia.

21

Line and Liza

To publicly liven up her show in Las Vegas, Line Renaud's manager had her travel in nothing but a four-horse carriage. But in the United States, everyone copies everything very quickly and soon Liza Minnelli was flaunting the same equipage everywhere. And one evening, leaving her song recital, Line sees the two coaches parked side by side.

"How am I going to recognize mine?" she cried out.

"Easy!" sniggered her manager, "*you're* well parked; she's got a parking ticket!"

22

My Kingdom

I dreamed that I was king. I had a palace, a throne, and a court. But where, then, was my kingdom? I summoned my Prime Minister to ask him. He opened a window wide and, inviting me to draw near, pointed with an enormous gesture to the surrounding countryside.

"Look at these fields, Sire. Not all of them belong to you. The first one isn't yours. Nor is the second, nor the third. But look at that one, the twelfth, all the way down there, almost on the horizon: that's yours, that's your kingdom."

23

"In Brief"

Dan Lochere, young hope of the Athletic Club of Saint-Mouezy, took his own life yesterday afternoon by throwing himself from a railroad bridge, just as the Paris express was going by. In a note left on the kitchen table next to his bowl of *café au lait*, the young boy explains that he lost his taste for life ever since his idol, Michel Jazy, retired.

24

Supplement to a Study by Marie Bonaparte

For years, the author of *The Raven* harbored affection as discreet as it was delicate for a little neighbor, Emilia Mill, to whom he wrote the so tender and sad *Letters to Millie*. And because Miss Mill had an utterly Victorian sense of propriety, he proved to be, for this period of time, excessively haughty and prim. It was only after the untimely demise of this sweet creature that his unbridled taste for the crudest porn suddenly came to the fore.

25

Half-heartedly

Answering to a wish wrested from him by his family on the occasion of an accident that he would not survive, an atheist agreed to convert.

When he was accompanied to the church and handed a missal so that he could sing a hymn with the others, his mouth, nourished by anticlericalism, sketched out a fearsome pout of disgust, but his lips read nonetheless!

26

A Fine Prank in the Belgian Army

The new recruits of a Belgian regiment are led to believe that at the conclusion of a long and particularly trying march, they will be able to quench their thirst at the Leffe abbey, so renowned for its good beer. But it's a joke, for the entrance to the abbey is positively forbidden to servicemen of all ranks.

27

How He Wrote Certain of His Books, 2

It is not accurate, as he tried to convince his early readers, that Raymond Roussel was indifferent when confronted with the external world and had never considered using himself in one of his plays that was given him to see performed.

It is known in particular that the famous episode of "La demoiselle à reître en dents"[5] resulted from a scene witnessed by Roussel during his stay at San Remo, in which one of those paver's instruments was equipped with articulated wings that allowed it to be hauled it up to the spot where it could be of service.

To a Waterway Disgraced by Mother Nature

Poor little rivulet, you are so ugly, so misbegotten, that there is really nothing better for you to do in this lowly world then go down there to have a good laugh!

Agonies of Two Serial Writers

La Malédiction du comte d'Ottlinger, the famous serialized novel of Anzieu and Harbourg, delights the readers of the *Petit journal* on a daily basis. But Anzieu and Harbourg, who write each episode in turn, sometimes have trouble coming to an agreement.

"If the Count d'Ottlinger is to have an unhealthy pallor and be excessivly thin, so be it!" thundered Anzieu. "But it's the same thing you wrote yesterday about the Count d'Hortaux. I won't have it!"

Harbourg tries to shilly-shally, but quickly realizes that he's in the wrong.

"It's true, I blundered," he finally admitted. "Let's do away with this character and figure out something else!"

30

Black Men Milking[6]

A black farmer complains to one of his friends.

"I'm having problems with my cow," he explains to him. "When I go milk her in my lovely boubou, she rubs her side against me in a friendly way, and my lovely boubou gets covered in dung!"

"Don't worry about it," his friend replied. "Just put on your loincloth when you go milk your cow."

31

Dialogue between a Lion, a Magpie, and a Calf

"For me," says the lion, "the cinema is just technique."

"No way," goes the magpie, "it's technique, but it's also art."

"Allow me to give my opinion," says the calf, "for me, it is only art."

32

The Example of Lucas

The success of *Tess* encouraged many producers to ask Polanski to direct *Tess 2*, *Tess 3*, *Tess 4*, *Tess 5*, *Tess Baby*, *Tess Strikes Back*, *The Tess Odyssey*, and *Close Encounters of the Third Tess*. Polanski is tempted, but hesitates all the same.

"What kind of story can I tell in all these films?" he asked the producers.

They answered as in unison:

"No problem, darling: if you want it to be a roaring success, all you have to do is center all of it on Montand who's shooting up!"

33

Factors Going into the Appraisal of a Parisian Brasserie

A survey revealed that everyone found the decor of the old brasserie Flo (passage des Petites-Écuries, in the tenth arrondisement of Paris) to be very beautiful except for, oddly enough, those who happen to be fierce supporters of happy people.

34

Conversation between Stockbreeders

"I don't understand it," groaned the stockbreeder, "I've five calves, but only one of them is putting on weight."

"How old are they?" asked the other.

"Well, that one, the one who's puttin' on weight, he's eight months."

"And the others?"

"The others, I dunno."

"Well then, it's obvious, you should know their age, seeing as how the calf with the baptism date is growing stronger!"

35

For a New Definition of Art

What is art?

It's when one fucks a Hellene serving in the Spahis (it's feasible, but you need to have balls ready for attack).

36

The Fall of Icarus

Why did Icarus fall? Because he got too close to the sun? Certainly not. Icarus had given the matter much thought and kept at a careful distance. But one of his wings demonstrated from the start an irrepressible attraction to the ground and this jeopardized his flying gear to such a degree that he ended up falling.

Two Pieces of Advice for Berthe

Build the county town of Lozère, and don't say that Eulalie completely crossed out her rough and predatory island.

TABLE

1. **LÉGER, UN DAN**
    [Slight, one dan]

2. **GUEUX LAID DE DÉPIT ERRE**
    [Beggar ugly from vexation wanders]

3. **LAID D'HERNIE, AI-JE OUR?**
    [Ugly with hernia, have I Ur?]

4. **CHEYNEY CHIANT**
    [Cheyney damned annoying]

5. **O, DEAL!**

6. **LES ANS FONT DU LIT MONT**
    [The years make of the bed a mountain]

7. **UN RUDE DIT VERS**
    [A tough one says verses]

8. **PIERO MONA MIT**
    [Piero Mona puts]

9. **LÈSE IO**
    [Injure Io]

10. **L'OINTE RUE «HEIL!»**
    [The anointed throws out "Heil!"]

11. **EX-HÈRE S'IL SE DISTILLE**
    [Ex-wretch if he distills himself]

12. **HONNÊTE YAOURT AU BONA FAIT GUEULER FAN**
    [Decent yogurt at Bona makes fan bellow]

13. **CINGLE, LAING, L'UN**
    [Lash, Laing, the One]

14. **LIN SE TEND, FAT AL**
    [Linen tightens, Fat Al]

15. PURIN, HARPO ÉTHIQUE
    [Liquid manure, ethical Harpo]

16. PAIX, TITE, COSME AU GO NIE PORTE HÂTIVE
    [Peace, Livy, Cosimo in go denies hurried door]

17. BATTONS SIFFRE, EH, L'ÊTRE
    [Let's beat Siffre, eh, Being]

18. L'EJUR N'A LUNDI MAIS SHALIMAR A
    [Ejur has no Monday but Shalimar has]

19. SI TOUT TIM A: GIN
    [If all Tim has: gin]

20. LADY MANGE DES LAVIS
    [Lady eats wash drawings]

21. LE SIEN A L'AMENDE, Ô LINE
    [Hers has the fine, O Line]

22. LE CHAMP DOUZE, T'Y RÈGNES
    [Field twelve, you reign there]

23. JAZY, DAN L'AIMAIT TROP
    [Jazy, Dan loved him too much]

24. SANS MILL MILLIE «HARD» POE AIME
    [Without Mill Millie "hard porn" Poe loves]

25. SA LIPPE LUT SAINT HYMNE
    [His lower lip read holy hymn]

26. LEFFE LEURRE BLEUS
    [Leffe deceives rookies]

27. UNE HIE S'Y TOUE, À REMO, D'AILES
    [A rammer kedge there, at Remo, with wings]

28. COURS RIRE, LAID RU
    [Flow to laugh, ugly brook]

29. UN COMTE HÂVE AUTRE? EFFAÇONS!
    [Another wan count? Square one!]

30. BAH, TRAIS-LA QU'EN PAGNE . . .
    [Bah, milk her in loincloth . . .]

31. LE VEAU LE DIT QU'ART
    [The calf says it's only art]

32. SUR LES SUITES TESS, ADDICTE YVES
    [On the Tess sequels, Yves addict]

33. **FAN D'HEUREUX, LAID FLO**

[Fan of happy, ugly Flo]

34. **LE VEAU À ÂGE ENGRAISSE**

[The calf with age fattens]

35. **L'ART EST LÀ SI ON NIQUE SPAHI GREC (BOURSES AIDENT)**

[Art is there if one screws Greek Spahi (scrotum helps)]

36. **MORT À L'AILE AIMANT TERRE**

[Death by wing loving earth]

37. **FONDE MENDE, D'EULALIE TAIS RATURE D'ÂPRE ET D'AVIDE ÎLE, BERTHE**

[Found Mende, of Eulalie be quiet cross out on harsh and greedy isle, Berthe]

these thirty-seven homophonic variations
inspired by thirty-seven titles
by Raymond Queneau
were made and composed
in the last weeks of the year
nineteen hundred and eighty-one

Paul Otchakovsky-Laurens printed
a little over 200 copies

receive this one with my best wishes
for nineteen hundred and eighty-two

TRANSLATOR'S NOTES

1. The n-ina, or "quenina," was Raymond Queneau's schematic generalization of Arnaut Daniel's sestina, a poetic structure held in high esteem by the Oulipo.

2. Perec's proverbs have been left in the sometimes awkward English in which he wrote them.

3. An abbreviation for *Roman Policier* (detective novel); to render the title as *Det Nov*, though, would have lost Perec's nod of the head to his publisher, Paul Otchakovsky-Laurens, known in the French publishing world as POL. Perec seems to have made a couple of errors on his list of authors (some of whom bleed more into the genre of the *roman noir* than the *roman policier*): William Goodis undoubtedly refers to *David* Goodis (whose father's name was William), and Horace McCoy's name is misspelled.

4. *Sic.* The title to Queneau's book of poems is in fact *Les Ziaux*.

5. "The paver's beetle to the soldier of fortune in teeth," playing off of "La demoiselle à prétendant [The young girl with suitor]," which produces the mosaic in the opening pages of Roussel's *Locus Solus*.

6. *La traite des Noirs*: "The slave trade," but *traite* can also refer to the milking of a cow.

WISHES

TRANSMOGRIFICATION

●

1970

A LITTLE ILLUSTRATED ALPHABET PRIMER

At the Moulin d' Andé

MCMLXIX

1

A British police officer announces his bisexuality to his parents by bringing his new boyfriend to a holiday visit. The boyfriend, amused at the awkward silence that greets his introduction, allows a dramatic moment to pass before turning to his lover's mother, widening his eyes, and uttering an exaggeratedly pert interjection.

2

An anti-Semite complains to his wife about a brashly confident Jew at the office to whom he had been generous enough to hand over a valuable client. Said Jew has yet to manifest any reciprocation.

3

John Dee and Edward Kelly were working through the Enochian system. Kelly, watching the movements of the angel's wand and calling out its corresponding coordinates to Dee, uttered a numeral that turned out to be slightly misread, resulting in the misplacement of a dash in the following phrase: Dee—Dido do.

Dee, remembering the passage from Vergil's *Aeneid* in which the legendary queen of Carthage kills herself, immediately echoed her act without further ado.

Kelly, correcting this minor yet fatal error some time after, realized that the message should have read: Deed—eye, doe, dew; an obscure enough suggestion, yet one whose inadvertent results had indeed brought dew to Kelly's eyes.

4

An Englishman not known for his wit managed to pin down the fourth tone of the diatonic scale before entering the men's room at his favorite watering hole and delivering his vocal calling card to those within: "Fee, fie, fo, foo, I sense the flood of an English brew!"

5

A drunken admirer of Gogol began to weep at the author's funeral, unable to stand the thought of his body putrefying in the grave.

6

The comedian Mr. Marin, cornered at a party by an avid fan, politely asks for his admirer's name. The boy, overwhelmed by such a request from his idol, stammers it out. On hearing it, Marin takes an interest in the boy's ethnicity, as he had immediately assumed him to be Semitic, but now has his doubts.

7

Louis—a low-down if not particularly intelligent, criminal—left behind two details for posterity. The first was his trademark habit of doling out caustic candy to little children. The second was the anecdote of his capture. When the police came for him, Louie took his father's advice to heart: When the authorities are after you, find some shelter and *keep a low profile*. After pounding at his door and refusing to believe his deep-throated claims that he no longer lived there, they found him in his bathroom trying to squeeze behind the toilet.

8

A child rushes to his mother to show her his new talking doll, fashioned after the most sadistic member of the Three Stooges. Pulling the string at its back, she begins to understand her son's perplexity when the doll, instead of singing the anticipated "Swinging the Alphabet" song, starts to moan like a cow.

The same mother and son watch Marcel Marceau performing on the street. After half an hour, confused as to why the performer has yet to move an inch, the child asks if it is in fact a human before them and not just a lifelike statue. She explains to him that Marceau's performance is being enacted in measurements of micrometers, which are perceptible only in the slight shiver that occasionally runs through his frozen and contorted body.

9

A man in a bad neighborhood chooses, as is his habit, a negative reply to the query directed at him; he does not, in fact, have any money on him. Watching the bent leg approach his face a few seconds later, he cannot help but feel that his life is becoming a little monotonous.

10

Hoping to add some spice to their drab home life, a housewife makes an opium-based tart for dessert. Two hours later, she finds her husband in the bathroom, sitting on the john with the most perfectly deadpan expression she has ever seen upon his face.

A paralytic's son suddenly realizes that his father wants something. Speaking to him as if his mind were no longer lucid, he assumes that his father needs to urinate, but manages to understand that this is not in fact the case. It is only after he confusedly goes to get his father's pipe that he realizes what is being asked for, and comes back to wheel his father off to go "poopy."

11

Lying back in his canoe, it occurs to the rower that perhaps it is not the Sun-god's *eye* that is casting light down on him, but rather, his *anus*. The idea of light being excreted upon him in such a manner, though, causes him to bolt up and continue down the stream in disgusted frustration, regretting the notion had even occurred to him.

12

An odd proverb, whose exact formulation has been lost, roughly states that a needle and thread is the best remedy for the disease known as individuality. The proverb's origin lies among the Dakotas.

Leaning over her secretary's shoulder to read her dictation, the executive has the mad impulse to impudently respire into his ear. He abruptly threatens legal action if not given immediate breathing space. She returns to her seat, brazenly suggesting that he do just that.

13

Before embarking on his directorial career, Jacques Tatischeff accepted a bit role in a never-released slapstick involving a series of gags upon a golf course. At one point, the director decided to improvise a pratfall on one of the golfers. Calling Jacques to the set, he asked him to affix a piece of string to the golfer's bare foot in the following scene. Asked to what the other end of the string should be attached, some directorial uncertainty arose.

"Attach it to . . ." Scanning the set failed to encourage any ideas.

"A tee?" Jacques offered.

"Yes, that's it!" the director cried.

"To a tee?" Jacques again offered, but his pun fell flat.

14

A son is informed by his orthodox parents that it is time for him to marry. He is flabbergasted, even more so when they tell him it is to be to the girl across the street—a nice enough lady, but one with whom he has never even exchanged pleasantries, let alone affection. His pleading questions are quickly trounced and, swallowing his despair, he begins to prepare for the ensuing courtship.

15

A Vietnamese woman decides to fulfill a pressing fantasy, which requires a voyeur to observe her in the act of fellatio. She places a personal ad in the paper, which ends up having an accidental, if not entirely inappropriate, typo: the "s" in "suck" has become an "x."

The typo that appears to conclude her ad, however, is intentional—a hugs-and-kisses that reads: XO XU. She wonders if anyone responding will guess her homeland through this inclusion of the former coin of South Vietnam; its low monetary value (roughly equivalent to the penny), gives a bit of a clue as to how "low" and dirty her demands are going to be.

16

Upon meeting the highly acclaimed Japanese film director, Raymond Queneau remarks to a friend how much the filmmaker's eyes resemble those he had imagined for one of his heroines.

TABLE

1.   BOBBY BI. BEAU: BOO!

2.   COCKY KIKE OWE COUP

3.   DAH: DEE—DIDO DO

4.   FA: FEE FI FO FOO

5.   GOGGY-GUY GO GOO

6.   JAW: CHEECH, I . . . JOE . . .—JEW?

7.   LOLLY-LYE—LOW LOU
        LAW! LEE, LIE LOW: LOO

8.   MOMMY! MY MOE MOO!
        MOMMY: MIME? OH, MU

9.   NAH—KNEE NIGH, NO NEW

10.   POPPY-PIE: PO POO
        PA? PEE? PIPE? OH, POO!

11.   RA, REAR-EYE. ROW, RUE

12.   SAW: CEASE I—SEW (SIOUX)
        SAUCY SIGH—SO SUE!

13.   TATI! TIE TOE TO . . .

14.   WHA—? WE . . .? WHY? WOE! WOO . . .

15.   XUCK—SEEKS EYE—XO XU

16.   ZAZIE'S EYES: OZU

GEORGES PEREC

1972

WORKED-OVER COMMONPLACES

[See p. 13–19]

1973

TRANSLATIONS FROM LATIN

"Dude, you calling us fat?"

He is calling them fat. He asks them how they feel about it.

"We're pretty unhappy, man."

It was indeed a strange summer: from nowhere came the black and hornless cattle of Scotland. We were all delighted.

Muhammad is on the airwaves, delivering a joke.

"This was only a test," he concludes. "If this had been a real joke, it would have been followed by the sounds of laughter."

Two boys preparing to shoplift suddenly recognize one of the sisters in their aisle—a sister known, moreover, for her eagle eye. The younger boy hesitates, his fear causing him to evacuate his bowels. His elder tells him to get his smelly butt in gear and finish what he started.

He's boasting about the length of his member. I suggest that he eat some bread soaked in gravy.

My palm was proving to be difficult to read, but she finally stumbled on a line that seemed revealing and started tracing out some of my past actions. But after studying them for a few minutes, she suddenly dropped my hand and looked at me with disgust.

A friend is describing his partner's skills in fellatio.

"For the most part, he's rather gentle. Sometimes, though, he has this brutal habit of using his teeth . . ."

I cannot believe he is telling me this.

"Well, Sal, what do you have for me?"

"It looks like they're watching over the body, sir."

"Ah. And what do you propose?"

"I propose we have something to eat, and then make a tour of the trains, sir."

Some days go by.

"Sal, I do believe you've been putting me on . . ."

"How much did he pay for these eels?"

"More than he should have—he got fleeced."

"Really?"

"Yup."

The eels flop.

"Put something over them, will you?"

Someone on the team interrupts the coach's harangue to inform him that the phrase is "eat to win," not "eat to wear." The coach looks down sheepishly at the vomit stains on his outfit, finding himself at a loss for words.

I ask where everyone is going. She tells me that the band "Cervix Wedlock" is playing a show tonight.

I couldn't help but exclaim how safe and warm her new flat looked. Imagine my consternation, then, when squatting to seat myself upon her toilet, I caught sight of the infection floating within!

We were watching the game; a player had just bunted and was running to first. For some reason, this encouraged the announcer to discuss an obscure etymology that linked the notion of the soul to the notion of the "substitute." I asked my friend whether said announcer might not be touched in the head. He replied that it certainly seemed so.

The tennis champ pauses: lob the ball back over the net, or take another sip from his piña colada? He makes his decision and winces as the ball recoils off his leg. A woman in the audience winks at him: it always pays to be pro-booze!

Citizens, when it is a question of our needs, the State is immature; when it is a question of our desires, the law is inexperienced; when our voices are raised, the courts grow ignorant;—Citizens, listen to my words: Ross Perot is a doctor of osteopathy!

I EXPLAINED THAT THE BIGGER DRY HEAT BATH WAS IN MY CAR. HE SEEMED CONFUSED, SO I TOLD HIM THAT YOKO ONO WAS THE GREATEST ARTIST OF THE CENTURY.

Given the absence of any grassland in the area, she decided to marry Gary Hart, her sun-bronzed neighbor.

It was a small man wearing artificial wings that delivered the horse. But he explained to me that the transaction was not yet complete, as I still owed them the tube that was lost when "my" horse had received her last suppository. Finding such a claim to be unfounded, I protested. He replied that if I didn't want to give them a hose, they would take a bovine instead: the choice was mine.

The professor, frustrated, has stopped using his student's names, preferring to number them through the anonymous title of "idiot."

"Idiot number four, tell me something about the Chou Dynasty."

"Well, sir, 'Chou' is what I called my big toe when I was a kid."

"That is not what I was looking for."

"I know, sir! Chou's a cabbage!"

"No, idiot, this isn't a French class. And if it was, you'd pronounce "chou" with a "sh" rather than a "ch.""

Silence.

"Hey, teach, I got a question: if I'm in a boat, and all I have is a bone, like a leg-bone, could I row with it?"

"Idiots, sometimes I think I'm teaching Greek."

"Why's that, teach?"

"Because everything you say is Greek to me."

I UTTERED MY DAILY CHANT OVER THE DASHBOARD OF MY FORD: "OH TEMPO, MAY YOU CONTINUE TO WANDER THE EARTH . . ."

THE SKY OPENED AND SEVERAL BEAMS OF LIGHT STRUCK THE HOOD.

Orson Wells redubbed several portions of Citizen Kane, *including Kane's famous opening utterance of "Rosebud." His original words: "Utter concern," seemed too obvious a moralistic lesson to inflict upon movie-theater audiences.*

We were holed up in Scotland, in a two-roomed cottage.

"Lock Benjamin up in the inner room."

"Yes, sir."

Things got complicated.

"What is it?"

"He was in pain, sir. We put some plaster on his leg."

I explained to Odette that the sense of smell can sometimes act as a figure of speech, in that it can link two otherwise disparate things—in this case, her lovely presence, and putrescence.

It was the final quarter of the game, and Gowen Glendower, known among hockey fans as "King of the Puck," was watching his shortness of breath manifest itself in pained puffs of steam. Before he could make the final shift into physical agony, though, the period ended. All he could think of was the smoking chimney waiting for him at home.

A bad influenza was going around: proof that our society was becoming hedonistic and corrupt.

My Italian friend, Timoteo, owns a sizeable collection of homes, but is up to his ears in debt. To make ends meet, he has decided to rent out his wife. She has several takers.

As he was being weighed in, it seemed obvious that the joint in his leg was not only scrawny, but completely lacking in strength. This explained why he rarely won any fights.

There was a whirring sound as I leaned forward and entered the tomb. I heard a moan—was it my father's aged sister?

She finished knitting the sweater and looked at the results: a profusion of "no's" were scattered about in no discernible order. Giving herself over to a negative frame of mind, she decided she may have gone overboard and tossed the sweater to her feline, Nil, asking him to tear some of them out.

TABLE

ABYSSUS ABYSSUM INVOCAT *ad augusta per angusta* ALEA JACTA EST aquila non capit muscas ARS LONGA VITA BREVIS *audaces fortuna juvat AURI SACRA FAMES* ave Caesar morituri te salutant CASTIGAT RIDENDO MORES *cogito ergo sum FLUCTUAT NEC MERGITUR* homo homini lupus IBANT OBSCURI SOLA SUB NOCTE *labor omnia vincit improbus LARVATUS PRODEO* mens sana in corpore sano NOLI ME TANGERE *numero Deus impare gaudet O FORTUNATOS NIMIUM SUA SI BONA NORINT AGRICOLAS* o tempora o mores PANEM ET CIRCENSES *qui bene amat bene castigat SIMILI SIMILI GAUDET* si vis pacem para bellum SUPER FLUMINA BABYLONIS *timeo Danaos et dona ferentes VENI VIDI VICI* verba volant scripta manent VULNERANT OMNES ULTIMA NECAT

GEORGES PEREC

1975

THE ADVENTURES
OF
DIXION HARRY

ALL'S WELL THAT ENDS WELL

After carting all of his money home from the bank, he went down to the shore where everyone was watching the crestless waves approach the town.

A STITCH IN TIME SAVES NINE

"คัน"

"That's correct, mom. Now give me a pronoun in German."
But she refused.

A THING OF BEAUTY IS A JOY FOR EVER

She cleared her throat weakly. They had gathered about her divan.

"Always be true to yourself," she began. "And never be afraid to provoke."

She paused.

"But let me tell you something, my children. Getting old is something to kvetch about for eternity."

TO BE OR NOT TO BE

She held up a piece of rubber tubing with a lump in the middle, asking me to guess what it held.

"A flavored peanut?" I asked.

She shook her head. I pinched the lump to get a clue, upon which the insect inside stung my finger and died.

ALL ROADS LEAD TO ROME

When the funny Jew came awandering to our village, we gathered about him and demanded he belt out a lyrical poem. But he just shook his head sadly and moved on . . .

DON'T COUNT THE CHICKEN BEFORE THEY ARE HATCHED

"Mmm . . . This is delicious! What's in it?"
"Well, there's flour, milk, egg . . ."
"But what's the meat?"
"Oh, that's beef."
"But it has such a different taste!"
"Oh, that's because it's mixed with chicken."
"But the texture is so unusual!"
"Oh, that's because I went at them with an ax."

IF AT FIRST YOU DON'T SUCCEED, TRY, TRY AGAIN

A stockbreeder, anxious about a shipment he was to receive, went to an oracle for some guidance.

"If the animals you receive have thick coats, then I advise you don't suck at the rye seeds when you masticate your bread, for such a response would not only be hackneyed, but dull. And remember: good things happen to those who go astray."

DON'T PUT YOUR EGGS ALL IN ONE BASKET

He was moping about the house, trying to dry an old shirt by slapping it from room to room with one of his golf clubs.

"Will you stop that?" I said. "Put it by the window, in the sunlight, so it can soak up some rays!"

TOO MANY COOKS SPOIL THE BROTH

The new king called for the general:

"Listen, you lackey, take your army through the countryside;—any screwballs you come across, I want you to bury them alive."

"Yes, Sire."

"And while you're at it, I don't like the air in this kingdom: I hereby decree that all air is to be sanitized before inhalation."

EVERY DOG HAS HIS DAY

"Have you ever tried interpreting a fart?"

"Yesssssss . . ."

DON'T CROSS YOUR BRIDGES BEFORE YOU'VE COME TO THEM

Victor took his bellyaching to a homeopathic doctor, who informed him that his stomach had twisted in upon itself. The doctor wrote out a remedy for him: a mixture of soybean, herbs, and juice extracted from a cow's spine, all blended into a hamburger.

"How am I supposed to eat that?" asked a shaken Vic.

"You just tell your teeth that it'll be an act of sexual mastication!"

LESS HASTE MORE SPEED

We were contemplating Andy Warhol's piss-painting, discerning a pattern in the oxidized streaks in the metal.

"There ain't no doubt about it," my comrade exclaimed. "He musta bin directing dair urinary-tract control!"

"So how do you propose reading it?"

"Well, let's start by assuming that he was working with th' Morse code . . ."

PEOPLE IN GLASS HOUSES SHOULD NOT THROW STONES

I discovered a tiny hole in the wall that allowed a view onto the women's dressing room. I had already managed to descry a foot and two buttocks when I received a sharp poke in the back. My kid sister was behind me, asking me what I was doing. I told her to scram. I was about to return to my voyeurism when I seated myself upon the musical whoopie cushion she had placed under me.

MANY HANDS MAKE LIGHT WORK

They were caught off guard by the cabbage patches: the crops were nowhere near the size they had expected! This did not bode well for their hands and knees, which were sure to be ravaged by the extra stooping.

MAKE HAY WHILE SUN SHINES

He asked his offspring to make a mound of petroleum jelly, but said offspring was too timid to even try.

EVERY CLOUD HAS A SILVER LINING

"You ever let one rip as loudly as the Earl when his tummy's in trouble?" he asked his companions, ogling Inge from across the room.

HE LAUGHS LAST LAUGHS LONGER

It would be a while until the girl's wounded buttock got better. She was lying in bed, sick, when her effortless appetite returned to drive away her symptoms.

IT NEVER RAINS BUT IT POURS

"Have you tried this body lotion?"

"Yes, it's nice, but it doesn't seem to tighten up my breasts or my buttocks."

A BIRD IN THE HAND IS WORTH TWO IN THE BUSH

One day President Lincoln heard a ruckus outside his window. Poking his head out, he saw the White House maintenance man engaged in a shoving match with a government official. The former was cussing loudly at the latter, only stopping when he had succeeded in pinning him to the ground. Lincoln asked whether such language was necessary. The official, taking his loss badly, complained that the handyman had spoken that way in order to unnerve his opponent and gain the upper hand.

OPEN THE DOOR AND SEE ALL THE PEOPLE

Oh surreal quill
May the dull sound of exotic money
Spill forth from your nib!

Cover over the crevice through which one spies!

I was teaching my Muslim friends how to play poker, stressing two essential guidelines: never relinquish the highest card in the deck, and never fold.

Things came to a quick stop, though, when Eve spotted a copy of the holy text and immediately began to recite some prayers.

TABLE

HAULS WEALTH, ATTENDS SWELL

ACED "ITCH" IN THAI, MA. SAY "WESSEN." NEIN

A THIN COUGH: BE YOU, TEASE. AGE: OY FOREVER

TUBE: BEERNUT? TUBE: BEE!

HOLLER ODE, SILLY YID! TO ROAM . . .

DOUGH IN IT, COW IN IT, THE CHICK IN BEEF. FOURTH: THEY ARE HATCHET

IF FAT FURS TO YOU, DON'T SUCK SEED: TRITE. AWRY A GAIN

DON'T PUTT YOUR RAG, SULLEN ONE! BASK IT

TOMB ANY KOOKS, SAP. BOIL THE BREATH

EVER READ A GAS? HISSED AYE

DONUT CRAW: SOY, HERB, RIDGE JUICE, BEEF, FOR YOU, VIC—HUMP-TOOTH 'EM!

LESSAY STEM: MORSE PEED

PEEPHOLE: ANKLE, ASS—OW! SIS, SHOO! DONUT THROWS TONES

MEN, KNEE, HAND DISMAY. KALE HEIGHT TO IRK

MAKE K-Y HILL—SON SHYNESS

EVER REEK LOUD AS ASS, ILL, OF EARL? (EYIN' INGE)

HEAL HALF-ASS. ILL LASS TILL A FACILE HUNGER

IT NEVER REINS BUTT-TIT PORES

ABE HEARD DIN: THE HANDY SWORE THAT, TO WIN THE PUSH!

OH, PEN "THUD" OR "RAND"—SEAL THE PEEPHOLE

NEVER GIVE ACE—A QUR'AN: EVE IN CHANTS

FOOTNOTES TO MUSIC HISTORY

1

Nikos had us over for tea. He must have sliced an artery preparing it, for the cups he proffered us were glimmering red! Maybe this was why he was unable to speak . . .

2

I felt like having a dark, strong beer; I mean, I felt like having another dark, strong beer.

They wouldn't give it to me.

I asked Hans for one, knowing he would take my side, being always ready to rise to the defense of an urge for a dark beer.

"Hey there, Hans! I want a beer!"

His being six feet under, of course, didn't help me any.

3

Perec was mouthing off and somebody socked him in the kisser. We split up, took sides, and egged both of them on.

4

Someone did a number two in the outhouse, so we thought it would be funny to lock her up in it.

Perec, of course, had to go let her out: not that she was suffering, mind you—she was complaining that she was *bored*.

5

As they were selling Joseph into slavery, one of his brothers began to feel slight misgivings. With some belated concern, he asked his younger sibling how things were going.

6

I told my friend that I had joined a gang: he was now looking at a full-fledged Wolfman. He looked at me incredulously.

"You're running with the Wolves?" he asked.

"Yup ... Why, you think I'm crazy?"

"Well, yes ... but then, I guess I already knew that. Anyone who's a microminiaturist has to have a screw loose."

7

A subgroup of the Luddites, named the Luddwigs (after the wig Ned Ludd was in the habit of wearing), was in charge of providing the entertainment for the Luddite get-togethers. Their favorite activity consisted in gathering in a circle (bewigged) about a defenseless oven and persecuting it, sometimes to the extent of biting and tearing at it.

8

"Karla, I simply don't want you marrying him."

"Then who or what *do* you want me to marry?!"
"Have you considered laughing gas?"

9

They took everything: his big palm leaves, his other clodhopper—even his parakeet!

10

I have an infallible method for crime prevention: when a thief enters my home, I tell him to go away.

11

What is less known about the author of *The Sound and the Fury* is that he was not only very wealthy but also quite physically fit.

12

I took my son to the fair. I asked the ticket man the price of admission.
   "Well now, we's got four prices here, mister—Ticket A is fer one kid an' dat's four dollah; ticket B is fer two kids an' dat's fi' dollah; an y'got yer ticket C fer a kid an' an aydolt, an' dat's sicks dollah'; an' a' course, dair's yer ticket D, an' dat's ten."
   "I see. And how much do we owe you, then?"
   "Well now, youse an aydolt?"
   "Yes I am."
   "One aydolt, an' one lil' feller, youse be wantin' a ticket C . . ."
   My son vomited.
   "But in yer case, it's a ticket D . . ."

13

Yes, this stallion descends from the deer family. One could make the claim that its lineage begins with an elk that proved to be particularly timid when faced with the advances of a randy unicorn.

14

I invited my aunt over for lunch in my new home. She asked me where I was now living.

"Well, actually, I'm sort of in a shantytown," I replied.

"In that case, I'll wear my sepia outfit—it should go nicely with those mustard-colored huts."

15

Someone has lost a sock along the edge of the ski slope.

16

I've discovered a remarkable cure for stress: I make myself comfortable as often as possible, and go to every wild party I hear about.

17

"Hey, youse th' dude dat rescued alla dose peoples in dat burnin' buildin', aintcha! Dude, dat wuz outtasight, man. Youse keepin' alla dose flames unda control 'n' all."

18

I had just finished building two oboes—both made from the dried flesh of a calf—when I let out a mild curse. I must have snagged them on something . . .

19

I was in the pub, nursing my beer, when I overheard a conversation at my side:

"Lemme tell you," a chap was explicating, "she had chimes on, and I mean chimes like you wouldn't believe—and she knew how to ring 'em, too!"

I asked him what he was talking about.

"I'm talking about knockers, son. Hooters! You know what I mean?"

I knew what he meant.

20

I was under the flickering trance of my dreamachine, ensconced in my tranquil domain of visions, when a power surge shut everything down, tearing me out of my reveries.

21

I gave Ian the house tour. In the parlor, my Burmese feline was mewling with my Tabby; in the kitchen, there was a heated hissing between Buttons, Sammy, and Henry; and a steady purring was emanating from the bedroom where my Siamese, Bagheera, was cuddling with the stray I picked up the day before.

22

They say we're living in times of plenty. I say we're living in times of crap.

23

We unloaded the shipment. To my dismay, there was not a single automobile. I asked the foreman how he expected me to get any tail if there was no longer a "back seat" to use in the warehouse.

24

Some people would call a cup half full—others, half empty. I say, fill it up to the rim and talk about something more interesting.

25

The captain's touching his mouth—drop the anchor!

TABLE

1. DUMB MAN, NIKOS—SCARLET TEA!

2. YO, HANS, SUB-BASTION: BOCK!

3. GEORGE FULL LIP—TELL 'IM, MAN!

4. GEORGE FREED HER: REEK-CAN DULL

5. JOSEPH, HOW YA DOIN'?

6. WOLF GANG: I'M MAD? AYE, YES: MOTE'S ART

7. LUDD-WIG FUN: BAIT OVEN

8. KARLA, MARRY A FUN VAPOR

9. FRONDS, SHOE, BIRD

10. ROBBER? SHOO, MAN!

11. RICH, HARD FAULKNER

12. GEE, YOUSE UPHEAVE? FARE D

13. MODEST MOOSE: HORSE KEY

14. AUNT TONED IF FOR SHACK

15. RIM, SKI COURSE: SOCK OFF

16. MORE EASE, REVEL

17. MAN, YOU HELD DA FIYAH!

18. HECK, TORE VEAL OBOES

19. BELL? AH, BAR-TALK!

20. SURGE BROKE KIF FIEF

21. OUR HOME CAT-CHAT TOUR, IAN

22. JUNK AGE

23. CARLESS STOCK! HOW SIN?!

24. FILL LIP: GLASS

25. FEEL LIP: DROGUE GOES

1978

ANTHUMOUS WORKS

1

What should one say to a girl exiting a bedroom, her face flushed, her clothes wrinkled, and her hair disheveled?

2

As we gathered for the witching hour, it was noted that the hole in which we kept our seaweed—the main ingredient to our ill deeds—was almost empty. I knew what this betokened: a strict diet of mayonnaise and our beloved booze served on nothing but chrome plates and cups. I could already hear our head witch barking out her orders:

3

Ask any Hindu mystic how one can pass through the closed portals of the Infinite, and you can expect the same reply:

4

She was accompanied by a man wearing a beret who was wielding a tome of Sartre in one hand, and a baguette in the other. I asked my friend who he was. My friend rolled his eyes:

5

A mysterious illness was overtaking the police force. Those of us not yet afflicted decided to raid a pharmaceutical laboratory for the requisite vaccination ingredients. We struck at night and plundered the joint.

Back at headquarters, my partner began to express misgivings. I had to remind him of our situation:

6

We were in my aunt's kitchen when a cockroach scurried out from beneath the oven. My cousin crushed it, hesitated, and then asked me what he should do with its carcass. I replied:

7

The doctor examined my wound. I asked him about the yellow crust forming around it.

"Is there asbestos in the building where you work?"

"Of course."

"There you are, then . . ."

8

I was worried that someone might ridicule the Jewish homeland. The idea of it actually made me sick: I got stomach pains. I went to see my doctor and described my predicament. His advice was predictable:

9

I guess you heard about Don? He finally changed his name in honor of his idol, Henry Winkler. If only that could have satisfied him! He had to go and try to fulfill his second fantasy: humping a male ox!

Ah well, at least I have this head cloth to remember him by. That, and a less than respectable epitaph:

10

The author of *Dangerous Liasons* was a renowned partisan of proper mastication. In fact, he often introduced himself as such:

11

Capone lays down everything in his wallet on the eleven. His moll, thrilled by the sight of so much money, can't help but exclaim:

12

Passion has no limits: unable to satiate their desires, Jim and Sue decide to surpass the sexual realm and try something new in their wish to commingle: they eat each other. They ask that their gravestone read:

13

I began noticing that every time she called him "lovey," he would start grinning like an idiot. I asked him what the story was.

"She likes to see me smile," he explained.

His explanation seemed to fall a little short.

"We have our own little code of love-rules," he continued. "Certain words demand certain responses. In this case . . ."

TABLE

1.   **LAY SHOWS**
       Les Choses

2.   **KELP PIT EVIL LOW? AGH! EAT ON CHROME: MAYO, FOND LIQUOR**
       Quel petit vélo à guidon chromé au fond de la cour?

3.   **AN OM: A KEYED DOOR**
       Un Homme qui dort

4.   **LADY'S PARISIAN**
       La Disparition

5.   **LAB BOOTY: COP'S CURE**
       La Boutique obscure

6.   **LAY HER OVEN ON IT**
       Les Revenentes

7.   **ASBESTOS PUSS**
       Espèces d'espaces

8.   **ULCER? RAZZ ZION**
       Ulcérations

9.   **DO BULL! VEIL, A SOUVENIR: DON FONZ**
       W ou le souvenir d'enfance

10. **LACLOS, CHEWER**
       La Clôture

11. **AL, FAB BET!**
       Alphabets

12. **JIM IS SUE: VIAND**
       Je me souviens

13. **LOVEY-MODE: DIMPLE-LAW**
       La Vie mode d'emploi

GEORGES PEREC

TABLE II

1. **LES CHOSES**

    Things: A Story of the Sixties, tr. David Bellos (Boston: David R. Godine, 1990)

2. **QUEL PETIT VÉLO À GUIDON CHROMÉ AU FOND DE LA COUR?**

    Which Moped with Chrome-plated Handlebars at the Back of the Yard? tr. Ian Monk in *Three*, Georges Perec (London: The Harvill Press, 1996)

3. **UN HOMME QUI DORT**

    A Man Asleep, tr. Andrew Leak (Boston: David R. Godine, 1990)

4. **LA DISPARITION**

    A Void, tr. Gilbert Adair (London: The Harvill Press, 1994)

5. **LA BOUTIQUE OBSCURE**

    La Boutique Obscure: 124 Dreams, tr. Daniel Levin Becker (New York: Melville House, 2013)

6. **LES REVENENTES**

    The Revenents, tr. as *The Exeter Text: Jewels, Secrets, Sex*, by Ian Monk in *Three*, Georges Perec (London: The Harvill Press, 1996)

7. **ESPÈCES D'ESPACES**

    Species of Spaces, tr. John Sturrock (New York: Penguin Books, 1997)

8. **ULCÉRATIONS**

    Ulcerations

9. **W OU LE SOUVENIR D'ENFANCE**

    W or The Memory of Childhood, tr. David Bellos (Boston: David R. Godine, 1988)

10. **LA CLÔTURE**
     The Fencing
11. **ALPHABET**
     Alphabet
12. **JE ME SOUVIENS**
     I Remember, tr. Philip Terry (Jaffrey: David R. Godine, 2014)
13. **LA VIE MODE D'EMPLOI**
     Life A User's Manual, tr. David Bellos (Boston: David R. Godine, 1987)

1979

PLAYING ON THE BLUES

Brief Anthology
of
American Jazz

JULIEN "CANNONBALL" ADDERLY

We were writing out a Dada reading list for our students when Julien spoke up.

"You know, we're forgetting someone important—maybe the most important of the bunch."

"Who's that?"

"The founder himself, Hugo Ball!"

"You're right! He should be first on the list!"

LOUIS ARMSTRONG

I was afraid he was going to break my toilet seat; every time he used it, he would lean with his weight to one side.

COUNT BASIE

Bartlebooth put his brush down and looked out over the water.

"How many bays do you think could fit into an ocean?" he asked his assistant.

"Five hundred?"

SIDNEY BECHET

El Cid's real name was Ruy Díaz de Bivar, but Ruy Díaz de Bivar's real name was Arbusto de Heno.

BIX BEIDERBECKE

Are you going to take that?! Give her a taste of her own mastication!

BARNEY BIGARD

"You could put a hayloft on him."
    "What do you mean?"
    "I mean he's large and he's tough."

CLIFFORD BROWN

He showed me about his estate: a precipice, the shallow part of a river that ran through it, and a hole that some animal had made it the ground.
    "It's all mine," he told me.

DAVE BRUBECK

My white lie of the day: I told them that the bumpkin had returned.

KENNY CLARKE

At this point, the water was pouring in. I asked mom why dad wasn't doing anything.
    "What do you want him to do?!"
    "Can't he give Noah a ring?"

JOHN COLTRANE

I was at the station.
    "Where can a guy find a toilet around here?" I barked to a porter. He nodded to a door.

I went in and groped in the dark, but to no avail. There was a sudden lurch and a rumbling. I lit a match: I was knee-deep in charcoal. This was no potty—this was a caboose!

MILES DAVIS

My sickly looking checklist: you see it as malevolent; I see it as the root of my strength.

DUKE ELLINGTON

The disease was believed to be incubating in the morning condensation: almost a dozen cows were already dying.

ELLA FITZGERALD

All of a sudden, she chuckled.
"What's so funny?"
"Jerry's here!"

ERROL GARNER

I set out to do what they asked and was about to start dragging the needlefish across the beach, when I realized that doing so made no sense. I asked them if I had heard right.
"Nope."

STAN GETZ

"What are all those smelly boxes?"
"They're my wood-dying sets. I'm trying to decide which one to use for the deck."

DIZZY GILLESPIE

In the course of a meal aboard a ship, a pea fell off of a fork, onto the deck, and into the ocean.

"And how came you here?" asked the puzzled lord of the Underworld.

"I drowned," replied the leguminous seed.

BENNY GOODMAN

"I'll have a bagel. Which do you recommend?"

"Sesame, dude. It's awesome."

COLEMAN HAWKINS

I could hear the coal-seller in the street:

"Coal! Get yer coal here! A dollar a bag, keep those ovens burnin'! Get yer coal! This week only, I'll throw in one of my kids, absolutely free, when y' buy yer bag a' coal!"

WOODY HERMAN

"Hey, when you're out, get some firewood."

"Firewood? You mean, like to burn up 'n' all?"

"Yeah. Firewood."

"Dude, you know how much that stuff costs?"

KEITH JARRETT

We had my grandfather cremated. I went to see the lawyer a week later, who pulled a small written document from a drawer: the final request of the will. I asked him what it said.

"He wanted his ashes to be locked up."

JAY JAY JOHNSON

I hadn't seen her in many years. She was now married with a husband, a young boy, and all the physical evidence of the time that had passed. I needled her and asked if this meant that she was now an old fart. She said she was, but placed the blame for it primarily on her kid.

PHILLY JO JONES

He asked me to feed his bloodsucking worm. I grabbed a vial and headed for the tank, but as I left the room, he called me back: I had taken some of Joan's blood by accident!

ROLAND KIRK

The Scotsmen did their logs-on-a-hill impression and then headed to church.

LEE KONITZ

His ice cream cones always seemed to end up leaking, so I decided to knit him an ice cream cone holder.

GENE KRUPA

He was wearing a new pair of denims and asked me how he looked.
"You've got your father's ass, all right," I said.

THELONIOUS MONK

I just read a very entertaining story—something of a cross between Christian Morgenstern and William Burroughs. After surviving a battlefield, a knee, enamored of its hero, the Lone Ranger, goes on a series of adventures before descending into a murderous frenzy.

GERRY MULLIGAN

A German was making some cider. He proffered a cup to his friend, a somewhat finicky British man. A slow sip later: "Better start over, bloke."

CHARLIE PARKER

He treated the poet as if he was some kind of servant: "René!" he would scream as he pulled into the driveway. "Put the vehicle away! Hop to it!"

OSCAR PETTIFORD

"Is the water shallow there?"
  "Beats me."
  "I'm going to go ask that lady."
  "Maybe you should ask her dog instead."

BUD POWELL

"Gimme a beer."
  "What d'you want? A Labatt's?"
  "No, make it a Budweiser—it packs a better punch."

SONNY ROLLINS

Dawn was about to break. We had been traveling all night and decided to stop at the next hotel. It was then that we realized that there wasn't a single establishment about that *wasn't* a hotel!

CURLEY RUSSELL

You want to make it in this business? You're going to need to know how to do two things: contort, and look like you're in the know.

HORACE SILVER

He told me about his trip to the red-light district.

"You walk down this one street," he said, "and there's a prostitute sitting at every window, with her back to you!"

"Her back to you?"

"So you can look at her tush!"

"I don't believe you."

"Honest!"

ZUTTY SINGLETON

I used to spend my time provoking drunkards, but I started feeling like it was wrong.

WILLIE SMITH "THE LION"

In William Blake's leaner years, he tried turning a profit from prophecy and hung a sign upon his home: MYTHS, TO LEASE AND TO RENT.

His first customer received a handprinted lithograph reading:

From the vales of Har, by the river of Adona, the loveliest daughter of Mme Seraphim is watching over you.

CECIL TAYLOR

My partner and I were at a second-class waterfront setup—a diver's dive if I ever saw one—working on the coral reef smuggling operation. We had been holed up for an hour when I noticed a lady leaving a trail of gritty residue in her tracks. I got a fingerful of it and gave it a whiff:

"Get on her ass," I told my partner. "I'm calling headquarters—we've finally got a lead!"

LENNIE TRISTANO

She showed up with a bandage around her forearm.

"What happened?" I asked. "Did Leonard try munching on you again?"

"Mmmm, I wouldn't say that . . ."

FATS WALLER

Two convicts are devising a plan of escape.

"We'll dig under that wall!"

"Are you kidding? Do you know how thick it is?"

"Of course I do: it's the challenge that makes it so appealing!"

COOTIE WILLIAMS

"I've got a whole troupe of schlock actors and nowhere to put them up. You know anyone with some extra room?"

"Have you asked that old codger over there? I bet he does."

LESTER YOUNG

Jung asked Freud how he wanted his martini.

"Stirred, not shaken," Freud replied.

Jung stirred away.

"But not that much!"

TABLE

JEWEL IN CANON: BALL—ADD EARLY

LOO HE HARM, SIT WRONG

COUNT BAYS: SEA

CID NÉE BUSH-HAY

BIX! BITE HER BACK!

BARN: HE BIG, HARD

CLIFF, FORD, BURROW: OWN

DAY FIB: RUBE BACK

CAN HE CALL ARK?

JOHN: COAL TRAIN

MY ILL LIST—A VIS

DEW KILLING TEN

A LAUGH—IT'S GERALD!

ERR-ROLE: LUG GAR? NER.

STAIN KITS

DIS: SEA? GILLESS PEA

BENNE GOOD, MAN

COAL-MAN HAWK KINS

WOOD DEAR, MAN

KEY THE JAR: WRIT

DIDJA AGE? DIDJA? AGE ON SON

FILL LEECH—OH, JOAN'S!

ROLL AND KIRK

LEAK: CONE KNITS

JEAN—CROUP: PA

THE LONE KNEE IS AMOK

JERRY, MULL AGAIN

CHAR—LEAP! PARK CAR!

ASK HER PET IF FORD
BUD POW WELL
SUN NEAR, ALL INNS
CURL, LEER: HUSTLE
WHORE, ASS, SILL: AVER
SOT-TEASING, GUILT ON
WILL LEASE MYTH: THEL EYIN'
SEA-SILT: TAIL HER!
LEN EAT WRIST? AH . . . NO
FAT IS WALL: LURE
COOT? HE WILL! (LEE HAMS)
LESS STIR, JUNG!

GEORGES PEREC

1980

ROM
POL

CARTER BROWN JOHN DICKSON CARR RAYMOND
CHANDLER LESLIE CHARTERIS JAMES HADLEY CHASE
PETER CHEYNEY AGATHA CHRISTIE ARTHUR CONAN
DOYLE IAN FLEMING ERLE STANLEY GARDNER WILLIAM
GOODIS DASHIELL HAMMETT PATRICIA HIGHSMITH
CHESTER HIMES WILLIAM IRISH MAURICE LEBLANC
GASTON LEROUX HORACE MAC COY ELLERY QUEEN
DOROTHY SAYERS MICKEY SPILLANE STANISLAS ANDRE
STEEMAN REX STOUT JIM THOMPSON SS VAN DINE

1

I am an herbalist and I roam from town to town.

2

A streetwalker I know makes a peculiar demand on her tricks: before renting a room, they are obliged to lay their genitals upon the hoods of their automobiles for her approval.

3

The bell rang and I dragged myself back to my corner, eye cut and knees nearly buckling. Raymond was there, Band-Aid already in hand. "You're a good egg," I managed to splutter.

4

My studiomate was preparing another one of his performance pieces. He had already applied a dozen or so leeches to his naked body when I espied some new faces among the usual bohemians in the gathering crowd. As it had been a while since I'd sold any paintings, I asked him to lay off the bloodsucking, afraid he might scare off a potential customer.

5

"Why is Jim hunting for worms in the pond?"

"I think it's time someone told you, Huck: Jim is suffering from depression."

6

We tortured him until he passed out and then discussed our next move: take him to the fields and turn him into compost, or fetter his legs together?

7

Don't worry, you'll recognize the old crone—she's slender, pointed, Germanic, and rather uncouth. And she's also loose in the wrist, if you catch my drift.

8

Well, you want to head home and warm up, or find another sucker to sweet-talk and swindle?

9

For my oral exam, I was asked to briefly describe a typical emperor of the Ming dynasty.

"Mucus-laden for the most part," I replied.

10

The king was given a list of earls allegedly comprising the "League of the Beige Order," an association of renegade nobles named for the garb they wore when carrying out one of their nefarious missions. Ill at ease, his majesty ordered the dining hall to be surrounded by guardsmen for that evening's supper.

11

I took the Roman god of the underworld to see one of my favorite films: Fritz Lang's classic tale of a child-murderer. Upon hearing the film's subject matter, my companion looked uneasy.

"What's the matter?" I asked him. "You got the willies or something?"

"Maybe just one little willy," he replied. "The film sounds a bit sick."

"I'm telling you, it's an acknowledged masterpiece!"

12

Two indisputable rules for the theater: violently thrust the heel of your foot onto the stage whenever possible, and *always* overact.

13

"Daddy, why does water freeze?"

"Well, son, once upon a time an Irishman was weeping, when someone came along and tapped him on the eyeball. Rather than stopping his tears, though, this tapping made them cold and hard, and they began to spread all over the world."

14

A game on which I am most keen
Involves both a king and a queen
Uses rook over pawn
And brains over brawn
You guessed it: the game is called chess!

15

We slipped into bed.

"You're about to experience what a Latin lover is capable of," he murmured into her ear.

But his pecker suddenly spoke up:

"I'm not Latin," it barked, "I'm Irish!"

16

The bigger the canvas, the less I know what to paint.

17

I enticed her over to me and seated her upon my lap. Then, to my great remorse, she farted.

18

She was not your typical prostitute: at once abominably filthy and bafflingly coquettish.

19

The devil offered her majesty an option: a trip to Hades, or a commitment to reduce her offensive odor.

20

Picasso often complained to his lover and model; especially when he found himself surrounded by yes-men.

21

A big-eared dame by the name of Minnie hired me to track down her husband: a rodent with a drug problem. I've no interest in pill-poppers, but she offered me a retainer that was enough to make my own ears swell. I calmed her down and headed for the bowery. Sure enough: I asked the first motel clerk I stumbled on if a rat had recently checked in. Ten dollars made him nod his head toward the stairs.

"Just follow the pills," he muttered. "They should lead right to his door."

22

In the old days, Stan would only haul goods around on a low cart by himself; but he seems to have warmed up to us—he now joins us whenever we're loading up a wagon.

23

On the beach:

"Come one, come all, and get yer wreckage here! Shipwrecks galore— we got yer chests here, we got yer portholes, we got yer rum, and we got all th' barnacles you could ever want! The best wreckage in town, folks!"

The most daring element of *Huckleberry Finn* was in the end edited out by Mark Twain: the discovery that Tom Sawyer's father was none other than Jim!

25

I asked Shaggy what he thought was wrong with the van. He looked up from under the hood:

"What's wrong?! It's on its last legs, that's what's wrong!"

TABLE

1. CART HERB ROUND
2. JOHN: DICKS ON CAR
3. RAY MENSCH: HANDLER
4. LESS LEECH: ART TOURIST!
5. JIM IS SAD: LEECH CHASE
6. PEAT OR CHAIN KNEE?
7. HAG: GOTHIC, WRISTY
8. HEARTH OR CON AND OIL?
9. HE IN PHLEGM, MING
10. EARL LIST: TAN LEAGUE! GUARD DINNER
11. WILLY? "M" GOOD, DIS!
12. DASH HEEL, HAM IT
13. PAT IRISH EYE: ICE MYTH
14. "CHESS" TORE RHYMES
15. WILLY: I'M IRISH!
16. MORE EASEL: BLANK
17. GASSED ON: LURE RUE
18. WHORE IS MUCK, COY
19. HELL OR REEK-WEEN?
20. DORA, THESE AYERS!
21. MICKEY'S PILL-LANE
22. STAN IS LESS ON DRAYS: TEAM-MAN
23. WRECKS, TOUT
24. JIM: TOM, SON
25. ASSESS? VAN DYIN'!

1981

DICTIONARY
OF
FILMMAKERS

ALEXANDER NEVSKY

AMARCORD

L'AVVENTURA

THE BIG SKY

HOME FROM THE HILL

CET OBSCUR OBJET DU DÉSIR
        [That Obscure Object of Desire]

LE CIEL EST À VOUS
        [The Woman Who Dared]

CITIZEN KANE

THE BAREFOOT COMTESSA

LES DEMOISELLES DE ROCHEFORT
        [The Young Girls of Rochefort]

LAST TANGO IN PARIS

THE NUTTY PROFESSOR

SWEET BIRD OF YOUTH

HIROSHIMA MON AMOUR

IRÈNE ET SA FOLIE

LES JEUX DE LA COMTESSE DOLINGEN DE GRATZ
        [The Games of Countess Dolingen]

JOHNNY GUITAR

THE MAN WHO SHOT LIBERTY VALANCE

LES MARIÉS DE L'AN II
        [The Married Couple of the Year Two]

THE GENERAL

IMITATION OF LIFE

NORTH BY NORTHWEST

GEORGES PEREC

LA NUIT TOUS LES CHATS SONT GRIS
[At Night All Cats Are Crazy]

OBJECTIVE, BURMA!

CLOSE ENCOUNTERS OF THE THIRD KIND

SINGIN' IN THE RAIN

LA SIRÈNE DU MISSISSIPI
[Mississippi Mermaid]

SI VERSAILLES M'ÉTAIT CONTÉ
[Royal Affairs in Versailles]

ADVISE & CONSENT

LE TESTAMENT DU DOCTEUR CORDELIER
[The Doctor's Horrible Experiment]

THE TREASURE OF THE SIERRA MADRE

3:10 TO YUMA

MICHELANGELO ANTONIONI

"Let the cunnilingus games begin!"
    The crowd cheered.

BERNARDO BERTOLUCCI

There was a scent of young women in the air. Having a fear of the other sex, the fellows decided not to go outside unless accompanied.

CATHERINE BINET

I was advised to lay down some bets on the baseball team, as they were winning so many games it was getting boring. It sounded fishy to me, so I made further inquiries. Apparently, the umpire had a hand in the whole affair, for there were rumors that he was the bookie paying out the winnings; not only that, but he was known for having a warm spot for informers.

RICHARD BROOKS

Susan's musical composition was classical in structure, but incorporated a rough, humming noise throughout. I explained to her that the sound made the piece difficult to listen to.
    "I could say the same about you," she replied.

LUIS BUÑUEL

Everything was set: we had been planning it out for weeks—his Tiffany lampshade was as good as ours! But somehow the fellow anticipated our intentions—he removed the lamp from the house before we could get to it!

DELMER DAVES

On a campsite, a man is telling his hard-of-hearing mother that they are serving dinner in the second tent.

"Mom! I'm talking to you!"

JACQUES DEMY

They dared me to sell my mute mother to the cannibals. Always a sucker for a dare, I took them on. We laid her into the canoe and pushed off from shore, the cook paddling in front.

STANLEY DONEN

Despite the sovereignty of the censor, he managed, via a cleverly concealed pun, to satirize the industry all the same.

SERGEY EISENSTEIN

Alan the necrophiliac went to pay his last respects and licked the urn when no one was looking. What he didn't know was that they had filled it with sand and left the ashes at home, knowing full well what his habits were like. What *they* didn't know was that he swiped a key to their house!

FEDERICO FELLINI

The conductor was trying to get the chorus to sing in harmony, but some guy's mantra kept screwing them up!

JOHN FORD

I proposed that we all made a gesture of scorn to the nasty man from the morning paper, who had taken a revolver to that nice lady who was fighting for woman's rights. I noticed that Valerie was craning her neck.

"You want another cup of tea, Valerie?"

"No, I was just thinking that you might want to put the lid back on the sugar . . ."

JEAN GRÉMILLON

In Greenland, seal meat consumption has declined, whereas that of bean curd has risen.

SACHA GUITRY

He is literally filtering the air; his chest is heavy and he is sighing, thinking of his aunt whom he had just met for the first time the day before. He sighs again, then comes to a decision: he is going to have her, one way or another!

HOWARD HAWKS

Suddenly, everyone in the next room was gathered around Howie. We went over to see what was happening, and I peeked over everyone's shoulders. My companion asked me what was up.

"Ew!" I exclaimed. "That's the worst case of conjunctivitis I've ever seen!"

ALFRED HITCHCOCK

I asked her why she wasn't purchasing the skirt. She replied that not only was it too small for her, but it was overpriced.

JOHN HUSTON

The prosecutor was grilling him, but he insisted that he had never been to the beach.

"Then how," the prosecutor triumphantly shrilled, "do you explain the presence of this tray in your apartment, thoroughly saturated—as every member of the jury will be privy to observe—with the briny odor of the sea?!"

Upon this declaration, one of the jurors was presented with exhibit A, the tray in question, which held the quite unexpected final nail in the defense's coffin: a flat and utterly modern-looking fish!

BUSTER KEATON

He landed a part in the film and acted like an ass.

JERRY LEWIS

Dean seemed irritated: "That Jerry! What a crazy guy! Did you know he's into heraldry?"

He was trying to sound jovial, but I could tell he was pissed.

JOSEPH MANKIEWICZ

She decided to name the comet she discovered passing through the lower point of Ursa Major after the eldest son of Isaac and Rebekah.

VINCENTE MINNELLI

He uttered a snort of contempt.

"He doesn't have the flu," he said. "He's just puking because he drank too much."

OTTO PREMINGER

You want a little corruption in your life? Start a real-estate scam and sell off inexpensive plots of beach property. Once you've collected enough money, send your investors a box of sand.

BERNARD QUEYSANNE

To listen to the song of the singing bird is divine.

JEAN-PAUL RAPPENEAU

Lacking sufficient virility, I relied upon a prosthetic member to satisfy my Scottish wife's desires. Unfortunately, the game got boring; to the extent that we reverted to a sadistic use of slow-burning matches to restimulate our passion.

NICHOLAS RAY

When the prostitutes come in, treat their tricks nicely; but if any of them starts roughing up my Scandinavian friend, he's going to get tarred and feathered!

JEAN RENOIR

He asked permission to go ahead with the experiment: a detailed observation of the effects of antacid on the condensed moisture gathered from a mountaintop. Permission was not only denied, but his salary was reduced, and all friendly relations between him and the administration came to a permanent end.

ALAIN RESNAIS

The guy asked me who the pretty lady was.
"What pretty lady?" I asked.
"The one in this room."
I looked behind me: Desdemona was in bed, riding Othello.
"Oh, that's my mother."

DOUGLAS SIRK

I opened the door and Doug collapsed into my arms, barely able to speak. I dragged him to the couch. Realizing he was trying to tell me something, I put my ear to his mouth.
"Whatever you do," he groaned, "embrace the truth. Avoid . . . avoid falsehood . . . avoid it if . . ."
Then he was dead.

STEVEN SPIELBERG

The count not only had a lisp, but was also extremely puritanical. So when he began getting to the heart of the matter before their conversation had even begun, his friend (a military officer) knew something was up.
"My friend, I nearly thinned. I wath almoth theduthed latht night! Thee wath in my bed: naked, luthful, lathiviouth . . . Thecthy!"

The officer raised his eyebrows: "And?"
"And, luckily, my penith came to my wethcue!"
"Ah?"
"Yeth, it wilted before I could act on my dethireth!"

FRANÇOIS TRUFFAUT

"Well, you gotta know my wife—she's something of an oracle, if you know what I mean. And when she found out about the extinction of the aquatic singing bird, she knew that the Day of Judgment was at hand . . ."

I didn't see how this explained the decanter of urine in the fridge.

RAOUL WALSH

"What are you kids fighting over?"
"This prickly pod!"

ORSON WELLES

They asked me if I was coming with them. I smiled benevolently and tried to illuminate them:
"To remain seated is the way to enlightenment, my children . . ."
"Then what's your walking stick for?!"

GÉRARD ZINGG

I asked Jerry what he had done to his lawn. It looked different. He told me that he was growing a crop of wheat: he had just bought a scythe and had put down a layer of manure the previous day.

I suspected that this was what accounted for his strolling about in such an agreeable manner.

TABLE

LOVE-VENT CHEW: RAH!

LASS TANG—GO IN PAIRS

LAY, SHOULD: DULL LUCK! UMP TEST DOLING END, DUG RATS

SUITE BURRED: AH, YOU WITH

SET-UP SECURE: ROB SHADE—DUDE: A SEER

THERE, EAT, TENT TWO—YOU, MA!

LAID DUMB MA, WAS SELL-DARE—ROW, CHEF FORE

ZING IN THE REIGN

AL LICKS SAND-URN, HEFTS KEY

OM MAR CHORD

THUMB MAN WHO SHOT LIBBER—TEA, VAL? ANTS!

LESS SEAL, ATE TOFU

SIEVE AIR, SIGH—MET, TAKE AUNTY

THE HUB? ICK: SICK EYE

NOR THE BUY, NOR THE WAIST

THE TRAY, JUROR, OF THE SEA-AIR: A MOD RAY!

THE JENNY ROLE

THE NUT! HE PRO-FESS! (SORE)

THE BEAR FOOT COMET, ESAU

HUMPH: RUM THE ILL

ADD VICE? SAND-CON SENT

EAR, WREN, IS OF HOLY

LAME, MARRY-AID DULL: LUNT

JOHN KNEE GEAT? TAR!

LET TEST: TUM, MOUNT DEW. DOCKED, TORE CORDIALLY AYE

HERE? OH, SHE: MOM ON A MOOR

EMIT A: "SHUN OFF LIE IF . . ."

CLOSE SIN (COUNT TERSE), OFFITHER—DICK KIND

GEORGES PEREC

LOSS SEA-WREN: DOOM—MISSUS SIP PEE

OBJECT-TIFF: BURR, MA!

SIT IS ZEN. CANE?

LAWN NEW, WHEAT TOOL, LAY SHAT: SAUNT, AGREE

1982

**QUENEAU
COCKTAIL**

At the OuLiPo
We prefer
The cocktails of Queneau[†]
To the quenelles of Cocteau

† A "Queneau cocktail" is a mixture of bitter San Pellegrino and Schwepps.

THIRTY-SEVEN TITLES

BÂTONS, CHIFFRES ET LETTRES

Strokes, Numerals, and Letters [partially tr. Jordan Stump in *Letters, Numbers, Forms: Essays, 1928–70* (Urbana: University of Illinois Press, 2007)]

BATTRE LA CAMPAGNE

Beating the Bushes [partially tr. Teo Savory in *Pounding the Pavements, Beating the Bushes, and Other Pataphysical Poems* (Greensboro: Unicorn, 1985)]

CENT MILLE MILLIARDS DE POÈMES

100,000,000,000,000 Poems [tr. Stanley Chapman in *Oulipo Compendium*, ed. Harry Mathews and Alastair Brotchie (London: Atlas Press, 1998)]

LE CHANT DU STYRÈNE

The Song of Styrene

CHÊNE ET CHIEN

Oak and Dog [tr. Madeleine Velguth (New York: Peter Lang, 1995)]

LE CHIEN À LA MANDOLINE

The Dog with the Mandolin [partially tr. Teo Savory in *Pounding the Pavements*]

LE CHIENDENT

Weeds [tr. as *The Bark Tree* and *Witch Grass* by Barbara Wright (New York: New Directions, 1971)]

COURIR LES RUES

Hitting the Streets [tr. Rachel Galvin (Manchester: Carcanet Press, 2013)]

213

LES DERNIERS JOURS

The Last Days [tr. Barbara Wright (Champaign, IL: Dalkey Archive, 1990)]

LE DIMANCHE DE LA VIE

The Sunday of Life [tr. Barbara Wright (New York: New Directions, 1977)]

LES ENFANTS DU LIMON

The Children of Clay [tr. Madeleine Velguth (Los Angeles: Sun & Moon Press, 1998)]

EXERCISES DE STYLE

Exercises in Style [tr. Barbara Wright (New York: New Directions, 1981)]

FENDRE LES FLOTS

Cleaving the Waves

LES FLEURS BLEUES

The Blue Flowers [tr. Barbara Wright (New York: New Directions, 1985)]

LES FONDEMENTS DE LA LITTÉRATURE D'APRÈS DAVID HILBERT

The Foundations of Literature (after David Hilbert) [tr. Harry Mathews in *Oulipo Laboratory* (London: Atlas Press, 1995)]

GUEULE DE PIERRE

Pierre's Mug

L'INSTANT FATAL

The Fatal Moment [partially tr. Teo Savory in *Pounding the Pavements*]

LE JOURNAL INTIME DE SALLY MARA

The Personal Diary of Sally Mara

LOIN DE RUEIL

Far from Rueil [tr. as *The Skin of Dreams* by H. J. Kaplan (Norfolk: New Directions, 1948)]

MORALE ÉLÉMENTAIRE

Elementary Morality [tr. Philip Terry (Manchester: Carcanet Press, 2007)]

ODILE

Odile [tr. Carol Sanders (Champaign, IL: Dalkey Archive, 1988)]

ON EST TOUJOURS TROP BON AVEC LES FEMMES

We Always Treat Women Too Well [tr. Barbara Wright (New York: New Directions, 1981)]

PETITE COSMOGONIE PORTATIVE

Little Portable Cosmogony

PIERROT MON AMI

Pierrot Mon Ami [tr. Barbara Wright (Champaign, IL: Dalkey Archive, 1987)]

POUR UN ART POÉTIQUE

Toward a Poetic Art [partially tr. Teo Savory in *Pounding the Pavements*]

LA RELATION X PREND Y POUR Z

The Relation X Takes Y for Z [tr. Warren F. Motte, Jr. in *Oulipo: A Primer of Potential Literature* (Lincoln: University of Nebraska Press, 1988)]

SAINT GLINGLIN

Saint Glinglin [tr. James Sallis (Champaign, IL: Dalkey Archive, 1993)]

SALLY PLUS INTIME

A More Intimate Sally

SI TU T'IMAGINES

If You Imagine

SUR LES SUITES S-ADDITIVES

On S-Additive Series

UN CONTE À VOTRE FAÇON

A Story of Your Own [tr. Marc Lowenthal, in *Stories and Remarks* (Lincoln: University of Nebraska Press, 2000)]

UNE HISTOIRE MODÈLE

A Model History

UN RUDE HIVER

A Hard Winter [tr. Betty Askwith (London: J. Lehman, 1948)]

LE VOL D'ICARE

The Flight of Icarus [tr. Barbara Wright (New York: New Directions, 1973)]

LE VOYAGE EN GRÈCE

Traveling to Greece [partially tr. Jordan Stump in *Letters, Numbers, Forms: Essays, 1928–70*]

ZAZIE DANS LE MÉTRO

Zazie in the Metro [tr. Barabara Wright (New York: Riverrun Press, 1982)]

LES ZIAUX

Eyeseas [tr. Daniela Hurezanu and Stephen Kessler (Boston: Black Widow Press, 2008)]

1

The Prof Is in the Pudding

I asked who the drunkard was. Someone informed me that he was a resplendent university professor.

2

When It Rains, It Pours

Peter went up onto the roof and I waited on the street. Pretty soon, a chap came walking by.

"Looks like it's gonna rain, doesn't it?" I queried said chap.

He looked at me quizzically: "It's a lovely day."

"But there's something in the air, you know? Like it's clouding over."

"There's not a cloud in the sky," protested this fellow.

"I see one," I persisted, "right there."

When he looked up, Petey peed on him.

3

Missionary Impossible

"I dare you to lie on the ground."

"You dare me to lie on the ground?"

"I dare you to lie on the ground with your knees up in the air."
"You're on!"

4

A Case of Mistaken Identity

"I just love your novels, Ms. Cheyney!"
"Actually, that's *Mr.* Cheyney."

5

First Reactions to Roosevelt

[See p. 108]

6

Fill 'er Up

The choirboy was slacking on refilling the holy water, so I challenged him to a duel.
The next morning: he's buckled over and groaning.

7

Air on Air

Just as the light went on, signaling that the commercial break was over, Eve belched.

GEORGES PEREC

When He Moans, It Pains

After Pete peed on him, the chap began complaining. From what I could make out, he was a Vietnam vet.

The Gods Must Be Horny

We all got into costume and started going over the script. It didn't look like my cloud role was going to involve very many lines. The guy in the toga started asking the director some questions.

"What does Zeus do in scene nine? I don't see any lines."

"That's his sex scene, buddy."

The Nose Flows

That was a rotten trick, Ann—screaming as I was drinking my milk!

Dust to Dust

All the carbon dioxide was making me giddy. When I came to, I was on the floor. I was telling the elongated dust puppy by my head that I now found it easier to breathe, but it corrected me: it was not a dust *puppy*, but a dust *eel*.

12

No Pity if Unpithy

If the speaker uses any figure of speech that you feel is overly trite, then start verbally harassing him. And remember, the essence of heckling is not in what you say, but the volume at which you say it!

13

Nose Transposed

A foul odor permeated the room. Everyone shifted uncomfortably except for Glen.

"Doesn't he mind the smell?" I asked a woman next to me.

"Well, his pants are on."

I expressed puzzlement.

"Oh, don't you know? Glen's nose doesn't work; he can only smell through the head of his penis."

14

Don't Try This at Home

Al tried mowing the lawn while standing on his head and gave himself a vicious haircut.

15

Marked Art Market

I feel bad for Ann; that inside scoop she got on the art market is costing her more than she bargained for. She's going to have a tough time making that money back.

16

Whine and Dine

While we were putting dinner together, we realized that the dog had managed to lap up all the port wine.

"Dinner's ruined!" screamed my mother.

"Not so fast!" I answered back. "Let's call Eve and see if she's got any tucked away somewhere!"

17

Play It Again, Clan

They were deliberating over the best way to conquer the enemy tribe. Someone suggested clubbing their chief with baseball bats, demolishing their village, and then providing the tribe members with not just physical, but also emotional pain. Afterward, when the enemy was feeling its worst, they would give them the impression that the war was over, when in fact, they would then start all over again!

18

Leggo My Leggo!

Ms. Mara was getting dressed.

"Those are some pretty sumptious stockings you got there," I couldn't help but observe.

"Sumptious? You bet they are! They're nylon!"

Upon which she poured her lovely legs into them . . .

19

Brave New Diner

We went to dine at Tim's Rendezvous, a fully automated restaurant and bar. The proprietor, an old Tim 19 model, greeted us at the door.

"A-tay-bull-4-1-sir?"

"No, Tim, for two."

20

Lead Astray

Her room was dominated by a lead gargoyle, a remnant of the now collapsed town church. It was in her bed, with the covers up to his elongated tongue.

"I felt bad for him," she replied to my questioning look. "He had no home, no one to love."

"Wouldn't a mannequin have been enough to keep him company?" I protested, my jealousy getting the better of me.

21

Allah in the Family

"Hubba, hubba! Is she delectable, or what?"

"I wouldn't tell her that, Ian. She's Muslim—if you want to get on the in with her, you should start giving to charities."

22

Ticket to Ride

Ian called up from his car phone.

"I'm at the gate. Let me in!"

"You're persona non grata, kid. Take off!"

"But my aunt's with me!"

"Your aunt? What aunt?"

"You know—the *opulent* one . . ."

"Come on in, kid!"

23

Getting Down with the Don

I was granted an audience with Corleone.

"Hey there, hot stuff!" He was bantering. "I trow[†] you got a problem you want taken care of!"

---

† A word dating from before the twelfth century: its obscure definition is "believe," its archaic one, "think."

24

You Barf What You Eat

I'm going to make you a nice, healthy meal, Millie: a bowl of day-old hardened cheese dip, and a ripe and fleshy pome. How does that sound?

25

Travels without My Aunt

We threw pebbles at Salvatore's window until he poked his head out.

"Salvatore! Come on—we're hitting the town!"

"I can't guys, I have to take care of my aunt."

"Forget her! Just jump down and join the gang!"

26

The Jungle Cook

After his bear-friend overate, Mowgli suggested that he lie down and get some rest.

27

Wars upon a Time

Gramps was going off again:

"In my day, we didn't have any of these newclear weapons, sonny—back then, we had real respectable wars . . . None a' these backstabbin' tippy-toin' 'star' wars, let me tell you! Back then, we decided things with a real gentlemanly contest, we did! Like, we'd select a couple a' little valleys, right, and the first ones to mow their valley won. Now that's a war, kid! That's a *classy* war!"

28

Gassed-on Leroux

The author of *The Mystery of the Yellow Room* had a mistress who liked him to talk lovingly to her buttocks.

29

Doting on Oat

After we had already finished counting the oat seeds, we were told to discount those whose shells were firm and sticky; those with prickly coats were to be attached together, like Velcro burrs.

Bases Loaded: Batter Up!

Camp Pinewood became known as Camp Panwould because of our old good-luck tradition in which everyone played baseball in the nude.

Cry Me a Moon River

"They just don't make songs like they used to. You know what I mean? This here, this isn't music—this isn't a song. Now back in my day . . ."

He rolled his eyes.

"Honey, I'm telling you something that's really important to me!"

Sewers for Viewers

In an effort to increase tourism in the city's labyrinthine sewer system, the government had gallons of a pleasantly fragrant chemical poured into its tributaries.

Up the Creek

They fished him out of the river. While investigating possible reasons for suicide, it was discovered that he had failed to adequately process his company's capital.

34

L'invitation au Bateau d'Amour

He recited Baudelaire as he stroked her face, all to the tune of "The Love Boat" theme song.

35

Putting on the Poor Man's Ritz

Tonight they honored a lovely young lady for having outlived everyone of her generation. Her alleged secret for staying so young is that ages ago, she was a German water sprite.

Her husband, Edward, not exactly a wealthy guy, took her out to celebrate and stood everyone at the bar a drink. The whole evening put him into debt.

36

Like Water for Air

I lay gasping for air, sucking at the oxygen mask.

"Albert," I sputtered, "there's not enough, I need more."

Albert went off and returned with a glass full of water.

"No, Albert . . ."

37

Song of the Celestial Wind

He then sang a ballad of that loving age in which our ancestors would climb the sacred hill. Upon reaching the top, the sacrificial rodent was consumed, and everyone's sacrificial gas set aflame; a rapid vibratory sound descended upon them, and they bent down to pray. Looking up, the celestial crane had lifted the veil of the everyday, and we saw the hill bared in all its glory!

TABLE

1. LUSH? SHEEN DON
2. GULL, DUPE: PEE-AIR
3. LAY-DARE: KNEE AIR: SURE!
4. CHEYNEY: SHE END
5. O, DEAL
6. LAZE ON FONT: DUEL. HE MOAN
7. ON (RUDE, EVE!) AIR
8. PEE-AIR, MOAN: 'NAM, ME
9. LAYS IO
10. LOW, ANN! DAIRY-YELL
11. EX-AIR CEASED: DUST-EEL!
12. ON A TOO SURE TROPE—BONE OF HECKLE: A PHON
13. SCENT GLANS GLAND
14. LAWN STUNT FATAL
15. POOR ANN: ART TIP, OWE IT—EKE
16. PET EAT CAUSE HOME AGONY! PORT AT EVE!
17. BAT ON CHIEF, RAZE, AIL, LET RUSE
18. LUSH? SURE: NYLON! TEEMED SALLY MARA
19. SEAT TWO, TIM-MACHINE
20. LEAD DEMON SHOULD DOLL-LOVE, HE
21. LUSH? SHE IN ALLAH: MAN, DOLE IN
22. LUSH AUNT? DO STEER IN!
23. SASSY DON—LEMMA: "TROW"
24. SOUND MEAL, MILLIE: HARD DIP, POME
25. SAL, LEAP! LOSE AUNT! TEAM!
26. LAY FULLER, BALOO
27. HONEST WAR: MOW DELL
28. COO REAR, LEROUX

GEORGES PEREC

29. UNCOUNT ROUGH OAT—ROUGH, FASTEN

30. BAT RAW: LUCK. CAMP PAN

31. LOVE OLDIE: CARE!

32. SEWER LACE, SWEET IS ADDITIVE

33. FUND RAW: LAY, FLOAT

34. LOVE VOYAGE ON CARESS

35. LAUREL LASS—AEON, NIX—POUR ROUND, EKE RED, POOR RITZ, ED

36. MORE, AL—ELEMENT: AIR

37. LAY: FOND DAY, MOUNT HILL—A LIT AIR, RAT CHEW—WHIRRED, A PRAY, DAVIT: HILL BARED

SUBVERSE

1.   *Pybrac*
     Pierre Louÿs

2.   *The Massacre of the Innocents*
     Giambattista Marino

3.   *Life in the Folds*
     Henri Michaux

4.   *The Thief of Talant*
     Pierre Reverdy

5.   *Wishes*
     Georges Perec